THE JOURNAL OF A GERMAN DOCTOR DURING THE WWII

Raluca Modreanu

*Dedicated to my husband who has always encouraged me
to fulfil my daring dreams*

*Dedicated to all the medical staff who are fighting with
covid19 right now*

Table of contents

CHAPTER 1

Siegmund's diary - Schleswig-Holstein, 12th of September 1939

It was at the beginning of my medical career when I had to take the hard decision to move from Berlin back to Kiel, because of my mother's illness. That meant leaving behind my research work at Charité Hospital, as well as, what I thought back then was going to be, a prestigious future in medicine. But I had no other choice.

Giving that the Second World War just broke out, I didn't consider bringing my mother to Berlin, as it had been probably my first option in other circumstances, and she clearly couldn't take care of herself anymore. In fact, I knew it would have been useless to suggest to her that she come to Berlin anyway. She was stubborn as a mule and she would never have accepted the idea of becoming someone's burden.

So I had to invent a reason to explain my return home. Starting a new job in a big country hospital near home sounded reasonable to her at least. She had never been to Berlin, actually she had never been further than the few villages near us, so she couldn't understand what I'd miss. On the contrary, she had always thought about Berlin to be a dangerous place for a young man like me. Even if she had never told me, a strict religious woman like her had always seen Berlin as a place of lust, where brittle morality rules.

What I felt most relieved about, was that in this way I avoided talking to her openly about her illness. Knowing her prognosis would have destroyed her faster than the disease itself.

My mother had raised both me and my brother, twelve years my senior, alone in a small village near Kiel, after my father had died in the Great War. Short after my father's death, my mother moved together with us to the house of an old widow, Herr Saft, a wealthy farmer, who needed a housekeeper. Herr Saft took good care of the three of us, giving us stability and even a good education to me and my brother. In fact, he treated us like his own children, giving that he had never had any of his own.

My mother wanted me and my brother to have academic careers and convinced Herr Saft to send my older brother, Hans, to law school when he was seventeen. My brother went to study in Kiel and, after he finished, got married and moved with his new wife to Dresden. We barely saw him after that. However, he did regularly send us money and eventually it helped pay for me to go to medical school in Berlin.

I had a quiet life in Berlin before the beginning of the Second World War. I was myself a quiet fellow, after all. Most of my colleagues were going out with girls savouring Berlin's busy night-life, whilst I preferred spending my time in libraries or just wandering the city on my own. During the summer holidays I used to visit my mother at the widower's house. I would enjoy swimming in the Baltic Sea, or riding my bicycle along the seashore, much as I had done as a child. When Herr Saft died, he left her his estate.

My best friend (actually my only true friend) at the university was Joseph, the son of a rich Jewish physician, who came from a long line of physicians in his family. Joseph was a quiet fellow too, and very ambitious. He was one of the best students. Because of the long family medical tradition, he already had high expectations for his career.

However, there was also another reason for this pressure he felt to succeed in life, which back then I didn't quite understand. While I (and certainly other of my colleagues, too) saw him as a ruthless competitor, his impressive knowledge and brilliant skills were, for him, the only way to compensate, in our eyes, his Jewish origins, and to receive the same consideration, as we others received, without doing any particular effort. It seems that whenever we meet someone for the first time, we unconsciously compare our own level with that person's level, and we do it, in our unconsciousness, so mathematically, that we know for sure that an high educated and rich Jew values more than an uneducated, poor one, but in the same time no more than a middle class, middle educated (or no educated at all) Aryan, and definitely less than his Aryan peer.

I wasn't aware how much Jewish families were struggling to keep a respectable position among us. I don't think I was naïve back then, but I had such a little contact with others, that I could say I practically lived in my own world, and in my world Jews were not discriminated against, and they shouldn't do anything in particular to impress me. Probably that's why Joseph was my best friend, without doing something particular, just because I liked him.

Joseph managed to maintain our respect and consideration very well for a while, that was until shortly before he was banned from coming to the university in our second year. It was then I began to notice strange behaviour towards him from some of my other classmates, while they were apparently still open with and friendly towards him.

One day, someone dropped the hint, as a joke, that he smelt - Joseph was rather obsessed with cleanliness and he often washed his hands for no particular reason, something I interpreted as a compulsion. On another day, one fellow reproached him for arriving late; he had in fact been the last to get there, although he did so no later than we had all agreed. It was also suggested that his desk was a mess, which would impede him from thinking properly. There were other similar small jokes and constant teasing, which at the beginning made no sense to me.

When he first asked me, as a close friend, about it, I told him he was being over sensitive because of the general climate at the time. Later on, however, I started noticing it myself. It got worse too, when his grades came back. They were noticeably poorer, without any explanation being given; the lecturers refused to talk about it when he asked them. Eventually, a short time later, he was expelled from university. I don't know if he really knew what had been going on, but at least for me, it was clear that Joseph's assiduously planned medical career was well and truly over.

The last time I saw Joseph was the summer after he was expelled, in 1935, when I invited him to spend some time with me at my mother's house in Schleswig-Holstein. We took long walks, or we rode bicycles together in the forest, which Joseph seemed to enjoy at least as much as I did. It was quite pleasant, because the weather in Schleswig-Holstein is never too warm, as summer in Berlin could be, but most of all we enjoyed the quiet. Even though sympathy for the Jews in my region was no better than in Berlin, there were days when we would lose ourselves in the forest and sometimes we didn't see a single other person the entire day. Everything was so peaceful and it seemed like nothing was happening outside our small world. I was quite glad that I could offer Joseph a chance to believe that nothing had changed, and that maybe when the summer was over, everything would get back to what it was before. But we both knew that this impression would just last for a very short while. In my heart I still had hope at that moment.

One of those days we took a break from cycling to enjoy my mother's delicious poppy seed strudel, Joseph's favourite dish. We were lying in the grass, looking at the tall oak trees, when Joseph turned to me and asked: "Tell me, Siegmund, do you think it's sad when an acorn, for one reason or another, never becomes a tree, according to the implicit potential to become one?"

I knew what he meant, but I also knew that he wasn't looking for my compassion; it was a philosophical reflection for him, so that I tried to give him an honest answer: "I haven't ever thought about it before, Joseph. I think it would be sad for that acorn, but it doesn't make a difference to the rest of the forest, as long as enough acorns become trees or at least a constant number of them".

We both looked at the blue sky for a while, without saying a word. There was such a perfect silence, that I could hear Joseph's breath. I closed my eyes and paid attention only to his breath, trying to keep the same rhythm with him. For a couple of minutes I had the impression that the time had stopped, but suddenly Joseph broke the perfect silence between us.

"But do you think it's fair? I mean, fair for that acorn? Generally speaking, I know it doesn't make any difference to the forest either. One can't talk about fairness when you think of the entire forest. If an acorn fails to become an oak-tree, it's just an incidence of a certain probability of things happening, that's all."

I picked up an acorn from the ground and looked at it closely. I had seen hundreds of acorns on the ground before; though I had never thought about their implicit potential to become oak-trees. To me, they were just part of the décor, and during my childhood, the perfect munitions for my slingshot. Joseph picked up one too and threw it far away. Perhaps he wanted to give that acorn a chance to find a more fertile land somewhere else.

"Who decides what is fair, Siegmund? Does fairness have the same meaning to me as it does for you, or anybody else? Do you think we can talk about an absolute or objective fairness, independent of someone else's point of view?"

"Probably not." I answered after a short reflection. "Imagine two people working in the same place, doing the same work, for the same wage, but one of them becomes ill and his physical condition doesn't allow him to keep doing the amount of work for which he was hired. If he worked less, and was paid less, he wouldn't have enough money to support his family. Of course, that's not his fault, nor his family's, that he has become ill, it's just misfortune. The other worker is very healthy and he might have the physical capacity to work more. Now, what would be fair: the ill person to keep working as he worked before, and die from it, or work less, but his family starve? Should the employer or the state take responsibility for him? Should the healthy worker work more to compensate, just because his physical condition is good? It's not his fault either that his colleague is ill. Fairness is not measurable or quantifiable, rather an agreement between members of a group, so that the idea of fairness could change over time, or from one group to another. But I guess everyone has his own rigid idea about what is fair and what is not, like fairness were an objective fact, beyond the human mind, which should be respected and followed."

Joseph listened to me carefully and nodded. "I guess you're right. I know you're right. But I still want to become a doctor, Siegmund, even if I understand that generally, for the rest of the world, it could make no difference. And I wish we were born with the acceptance of failure when things can't be changed. Why are we made to grieve for something we can't have? I feel rational and irrational at the same time. If Darwin was right, then the one who carries inside the potential to succeed should also fight for it, but the others should just accept their fate. Otherwise, what's the point? Why struggle for something you can never achieve, especially when you rationally know it, and understand it too? It is just a waste of energy!"

I didn't know what to say, but he continued: "People denied or even hated religion for its wars and unfairness, but I hate Darwin and Nietzsche. I know now that I'm not and I'll never be an "Übermensch""

"Now you're irrational." I said and I smiled at him. "I think neither Darwin, nor Nietzsche, were thinking that we'd come to this; you can't blame them for something they didn't think of."

"That's the point."

The next day Joseph was gone without having said anything to me about his intentions. I hoped he had left a good-bye note at least, but there was none. There was just an acorn on my desk, he had probably picked up from the wood the day before. Since that day I've always carried along Joseph's acorn in my pocket.

CHAPTER 2

Siegmund's diary - Schleswig-Holstein, 1st of October 1939

I was haunted by these memories of Joseph, reflecting on how his promising future in medicine had been prematurely and irreversibly cut off by an unexpected twist of political regime, whilst waiting in a small and dark anteroom to meet my future Chefarzt. It was my first day of work in a country hospital. I didn't feel nervous at all, not like I would have felt in a similar situation in Berlin. Maybe that was because in Berlin I'd always felt a little bit like the country boy who had come to live in a big city, and now my perception, coming back from the capital to my hometown, was exactly the opposite. Studying and working for a while in a prestigious hospital in Berlin gave me a certain feeling of superiority towards my new colleagues, whose medical experience was limited to their work in a former sanatorium. I've never been a conceited guy, at least this has never been my perception about myself, but I guess there are circumstances that give us a superiority complex, without even being aware of it. Or maybe the excitement of my new position was lacking, because I expected my future job to be kind of routine. I already missed Berlin, and most of all Joseph. I missed our long talks and the ideas that emerged from them. We had also shared the same interest in research, given that his father, an eminent professor of microbiology, had introduced both of us to the field. I just hopped, someday, it would be possible to go back to my academic career again. And who knows, maybe, one day, I would meet Joseph again too.

Meanwhile, I just had to readapt to what my life had been before moving to Berlin. That included the rain, the almost constant rain, which had never bothered me before, but curiously, seemed to bother me now. I stood up and I looked through a small window into the hospital's back garden. It was November, but the grass was still green because of the continuous drizzle. I opened the window and I inhaled the fresh chilli air. It wasn't so bad, after all. It reminded me of my childhood, playing with other boys outside, despite the chill and the mud. We actually used the mud as the precious material for building our fortresses, or for simply throwing at each other. I wished I had that joy for simple things again.

I closed the window and suddenly realized that my future Chefarzt's secretary was standing behind me, not saying anything. She was a middle-aged woman, modestly dressed, and without the makeup all the secretaries in Berlin used to wear. Somehow, I found that comforting. My mother had never worn makeup either. I greeted her by inclining slightly my head.

"Herr Adler is waiting for you, Herr Berg.", she said with a feeble voice. Then, as she had found it inappropriate to be stood behind me without saying a word, she added: "I saw that you needed some fresh air, and I didn't want to bother you." She continued in a more familiar way: "Don't worry, Herr Berg, Herr Adler is a jovial friendly man. It's very easy to work with him. I guess you are used to different kind of relationship with your superiors in Berlin. Here we are more like a big family."

"I'm not worried." I answered with a smile. "I was just reminding of my childhood and wanted to inhale the friendly, wet, windy air of Schleswig-Holstein again." I said, trying to sound jovial too. But she didn't smile back, as she didn't like my joke, or maybe she didn't understand it. I guess for someone who has always lived in that wet and windy atmosphere there was nothing to joke about; there was just the air she breathed in every day. Without adding anything, she turned on her heels, and I followed her to Herr Adler's office.

"Ah, Herr Berg", a big man with a kind smile greeted me from behind his desk. He rose up and shook my hand vigorously. "Adler is my name, but I guess you already know that. Welcome, I've heard only great things about you. You did excellent work at Charité, didn't you?" and then offered me a seat.

Herr Adler's office was very big and decorated with nice pieces of furniture which looked very expensive to me. It made an odd contrast with the general poverty, especially in that lost village. However, Herr Adler fitted in his office very well. He was a charming confident man, with an aristocratic look, who reminded me of some of my superiors in Berlin. As he had read my thoughts, he said cheerfully:

"You know, I worked in Berlin for Charité too. For many years actually. What a great time I had there! Great colleagues, great work, and most of all, great mentors! I have some fond memories of it." Then he suddenly became thoughtful. "But I had to go, you know, when the political situation changed. We, doctors, shouldn't be involved in politics; it is not our business. And I couldn't avoid it in Berlin. At least I am my own master here, in this small village." Then he changed the subject trying to look cheerful: "Have you found a good place to stay here? I could arrange something for you, if you like."

"I'm living with my mother, who lives ten kilometres from here. She's ill and I have to take care of her, but I can be here in half an hour by bicycle."

"Oh, yes, I remember now! Professor Reichmann mentioned something about your mother in his recommendation letter, before he sent you to me. I believe your mother has a heart failure, if I remember well, hasn't she?"

"Yes, she gets tired quickly even making the smallest efforts. I believe she has a heart failure. Her blood pressure is also too low." I responded vaguely.

"You know that you can bring her here, if you want to. We have an excellent cardiologist who could give you his opinion. Besides, in case anyone wants to send you to the Front, it's good to have an official statement that says your mother is in poor health and you're the only one who can take care of her. Tell me if I can do anything for you or your mother; medicines are also hard to find these days. Anyway, Professor Reichmann also wrote that you're an excellent, ambitious, hard-working young fellow with a lot of potential, and that one day, when this damned war is over, you'll become someone. 'A great name in the history of medicine', were his exact words, Herr Berg. You've really impressed him - a great name in the history of medicine, that's something. I should say I feel proud too to have someone like you here. Welcome."

Then his enthusiasm changed again to gloominess. I discovered in time that these sudden mood changes were a part of his personality. He looked long into my eyes: "I think I can guess what you're feeling. You're thinking that coming to us wouldn't have been your first option. I felt the same when I arrived here. You'll get used to it, though. It's not so bad, you'll see. At least here you can see other cases, other than wounded soldiers, and you'll soon appreciate that, I'm sure. Besides, I'll take good care of you, as I promised Professor Reichmann. This war has torn us apart, but don't lose morale."

That afternoon, on my way home, I picked up some flowers for my mother. "Otto, is that you?" cried my mother from the kitchen, when she heard me opening the door.

"No, mother, it's me, Siegmund."

"Is Otto with you?"

"No mother, I'm alone."

"Where is he then? He knows how much I hate it when he's late. I hope he hasn't forgotten to bring me that soap I told him about this morning. I've been cooking for him the entire day, cleaning the house, and he's late! In the company of those Jews, those devils, he has forgotten what punctuality means. They just lie and steal from us. I know how they are! They can fool you, but they won't fool me. Otto is such a fool! If he keeps doing business with them, they will ruin us one day! Look at this house; we're poor, we've never been this poor before, where is our stuff? I barely found anything in the kitchen to cook for today!" said my mother lifting her arms to the ceiling, as if she wanted to threaten some unfair and malicious Gods with her fists. "I warned him last night: don't let yourself be fooled by those devils, because they are thieves, those communists! Not to mention the French, too! You can never trust them! They stole Alsace-Lorraine from us, our land, and humiliated us! Von Bismarck's wife was right; he should have let them all be killed, women and children too. She was right! I keep telling Otto: you can never trust the French. They're filthy, lazy, and they're always late. You can't trust someone who's late, and I know what I'm talking about. Where is this country going to? What is that, a republic? Our great Prussia is now a Republic! They stole our land and our dignity with it, those devils! How could they dare humiliate us? And Otto, a naïve fool, is still doing business with them, in spite of it all. Where is he now? Did he tell you when he's coming home tonight? Has he forgotten that he has a home and a family?"

I put the flowers in a glass and I kissed her forehead. "Mother, papa isn't coming back. He died 24 years ago, a few months after I was born, remember? Now it's 1939, and war again." And I realized sadly that her psychotic wishes were true. We weren't a Republic anymore, but an expanding Reich.

CHAPTER 3

Siegmund's diary - Schleswig-Holstein, October-November 1939

Since we were just a few doctors in the hospital, I was responsible for forty beds, which were always full with patients. The poverty that the great depression had brought in the 1930s was resented especially in the countryside, where because of malnutrition, and the lack of resources, many children and old people were always catching infections. It got even worse after the Second World War broke out. Soldiers brought home new forms of influenza, so that everybody, even the ones who weren't directly involved in the war, experienced new forms of coughs and diarrhoeas.

I worked from 6 am to 8 pm every day, and when I arrived home I was normally so tired that I could barely talk with my mother, which, since she had been alone all day, caused her a lot of frustration. I kept observing that her mental status fluctuated, so that sometimes she could be very lucid, but sometimes she seemed to live in a whole different world to mine. I tried to keep her informed all the time about new political events, as well as my day-to-day life at the hospital, which gave her much pleasure.

Sometimes she asked me about other little details that interested her for some reason. She was particularly interested to know if there was someone at my hospital, a female someone, with whom I could form a family. She was also very direct about the subject and spoke her mind, exactly how I had known her before she became ill. "Siegmund, are you sure there's nobody there who catches your eye? You are a young, good looking man and a doctor too! I'm sure you are a good catch for most of those women you are working with! And don't forget, with this war, there aren't so many men here anymore. When I think of it, I could almost say it's a waste, what you are doing. A waste for you, a waste for me and a waste for those women too! I want to see my grandchildren grow up, whilst I'm still alive… Don't think about me, Siegmund, I can still take care of myself, you know. Look! Your brother was already married when he was twenty-one, and at your age he had already had two children!"

My brother Hans was always, in my mother's eyes, the model I should follow, although we barely saw him; once a year at best, when he came with his family to visit us. I don't think my mother knew very well what my brother had been doing with his life since he had left home, but she had built up such a good image of him, in her head, that no matter what he was really doing, hundreds of kilometres away, his image was indestructible.

My mother used to talk a lot about Hans, but even more about my father. She wanted to keep his memory alive to us. Even though I never met my father, the detailed stories my mother told me helped me to have a very clear image of him. I imagined my father was like a super-hero: strong, brave and kind. He fought like a lion and was always there for his comrades whenever they were in trouble. He had a hard surface, but a soft core. When I grew older, I realized that the super-hero image my mother had created was probably an idealized one too, like the one of my brother. We had one photo of my father, dressed in his uniform, which my mother kept on a marble console table, the most precious piece of furniture we had in our house. My mother always looked at that photo with great affection.

"Your father died when you were very young, but I have you two. And even if he is dead, you two are here, carrying on his name and his blood. I'm sure that if he had had time to think of something before he died, he must have thought about you. Do you know what he wrote to me from the Front once? That if there was anything he would deeply regret, if he died, it was that he had had no opportunity to get to know you and spend some time with you. After you were born, his biggest wish was to come home and meet you. 'Whatever that boy does, tell him that I'm proud of him and I wish I had met him'. That is what he wrote to me. A family is the best thing one can have, so do yourself a favour and have one!"

My mother was indeed right, regarding the interest women had in me, and given the context, I was probably the best candidate for most of them, not because I really had something special to offer them, but rather because of the lack of men around, especially young unmarried ones, like myself. I was treated daily to home-made cakes or at least big smiles, which made my work very pleasant, up to a certain point. I could say I generally enjoyed my work. The war made us warm to each other and since many families were separated, we were like a big family together. We shared our hopes and fears and we knew everything about each other's lives. In our free time we played games or organized dancing-tea meetings, where sometimes patients or even soldiers on leave from their units, took part too.

There were patients who came to us, especially the older ones, not because they were genuinely ill, but because they were lonely at home and looking for company. Many of them invented something to convince us to admit them to the hospital. One of them was Herr Müller. Herr Müller came all the time, and since he had a fabulous imagination, always invented new symptoms to convince us. The young doctors or nurses always believed him, which caused him a great personal satisfaction. After so many years and a lot of time spent at the hospital he seemed to have better medical knowledge than the personal that had just started to work with us.

He also enjoyed mocking other patients, the ones he shared a room with, by simulating a heart attack or stomach ache in the middle of the night; crying out so loud for help that nobody, neither patients nor personal, could rest. Soldiers, especially, were furious about his mockery and some of them pretended that they were anxious to go back to their units, where they could sleep better, though nobody truly believed them either. In spite of that, everyone loved Herr Müller, because his presence among us made us forget about our worries or deeply hidden sadness, and even though he received a lot of scolding from the nurses, he competed with me when it came to home-made cakes and smiles. Somehow, he reminded me of Herr Saft, so I was fond of him too. That's why I never sent him home on my shifts, when he came in with his well-known theatrics to be admitted to our hospital again.

"You're a good young man. I know that you're smart enough to recognize my little charades, but you still let me in every time." he said to me with great fondness. "But listen to me, being too warm-hearted will cause you problems. You take life too seriously, I'm afraid. Look at me! I'm an old man, mocking everyone, and I'm still doing great, not to mention the fact that I receive and eat more cookies than you do! People need loud-mouth clowns more than they need a good heart. If I weren't a clown, I'd be just a useless old man. There's nothing that people enjoy more than being entertained with foolish charades and phony fuss, if those bring them together and give them the illusion that they belong to each other. Don't get too isolated from the rest, or you'll lose the game.

We're nothing but social animals. I'm a wise man, as you can see". And he winked.

I felt a little embarrassed, which I felt every time a patient seemed to dominate me in the conversation, even if it wasn't done with any bad intentions, as was the case with Herr Müller. But since I was still a young doctor and not completely confident in myself and my own image, I wasn't at ease with the conversation. Since I had started practising as a physician, I felt that my white gown gave me a certain superiority, like white protection which stood between the real me and the rest, even if I wasn't conscious of it. And when someone gave me advice, despite my exalted position in the doctor-patient relationship, I took it rather personally, as if I had done something wrong, which revealed to others what a naïve young man I was, instead of an experienced doctor. After all, I could have sent him home, since he wasn't actually ill, and it was within my power to do that, but he was right, and probably I had a good heart, as he had said to me, so I forgave him anyway.

Besides Herr Müller, one of the most emblematic figures at our hospital was Nurse Frieda. She was only two years older than me, but the veteran at our hospital, as she had been working there since she was sixteen, long before the war had begun. Frieda was very skilful, efficient and reliable, not to mention very organized and level-headed, in a nutshell, everything we needed in those chaotic times. She was extremely devoted to her work and patients, knew every procedure, remained calm in emergency situations, when everyone else panicked, which made her very well thought of by us all. Frieda was our friend, sister, mother, confidante and counsellor. Even when she sometimes bossed everyone around and gave us all orders, we tacitly accepted it, because somehow all of us, medical staff and patients, recognized her as the foundations that kept the house standing and that it seemed only natural to obey her orders.

She spent the entire time at the hospital; at least she was always there when I came to work and still there when I went home. She had her house near the hospital, but I bet there were days when she never went home, or maybe just to take a bath or change her clothes. Although she was married and her husband was fighting in the war, it seemed that they didn't get along and sometimes we heard her saying "If that son of a bitch never came back, I wouldn't give a damn!" Nobody knew if she was serious about that, or if was just a bluff, because she always tried to keep up the image of a tough woman, whose feelings weren't affected too much, assuming she really had any. She also smoked a lot and always had an extra packet of cigarettes for soldiers.

Frieda also had enormous breasts and there were rumours that she was more than generous with our soldier patients, offering them the opportunity to peep at her when she was changing her clothes (always accidentally, of course), before they were discharged from us and sent back to their units. It seemed that this act of benevolence gave her great satisfaction, knowing that she could be the last naked woman they would see in their short lives, like a last meal given to a convicted man before his execution. Somehow, this gave her a certain feeling of fulfilment, as if only then would her duty toward them be fulfilled.

The only one who was really intrigued and disappointed at the same time about that was our Herr Müller. Despite his repeated attempts to convince her that he was also going to die soon, it seemed that Frieda was merciless with him and didn't offer him any satisfaction. "I don't get it!" Herr Müller kept saying to me. "The odds that I could die soon are surely greater than any other man around. I'm an old man, so I will die. Isn't that obvious to her? What is she waiting for? For me to really have a heart attack?" But for Frieda, there was a big difference when it came to differentiating between the young men who bravely fought for their country, and an old fool who only played charades. Some cheeky nurses even gossiped that Frieda was doing her little favours in the hope that she would make her husband jealous, because one of those young soldiers might be one of his comrades. "Don't worry, Herr Müller," I sometimes tried to comfort him, "she hasn't shown them to me either". "What do you need to see them for? You're a doctor, for Christ's sake!" he mumbled grumpily and I always laughed. But it was true; Frieda didn't show any particular interest in me, except in our working relationship and certain sympathy as a friend.

CHAPTER 4

Siegmund's diary - Schleswig-Holstein, December 1939-January 1940

Despite the general situation, our life in that lost village still followed normality, though of course only up to a certain point. We did notice the lack of resources, especially of food and medicines, and also the lack of young men to do the hard work, though women managed to replaced their presence pretty well. There were fewer babies or small children to be seen around, but we constantly had our little patients, since poorer nutrition and new types of influenza made them prone to disease more often. I loved working with children because of their innocence, in spite of the constant propaganda in the press, on the radio or in schools.

Actually, in our village just a few people had radios at home and the majority were too busy to read the press and teachers in schools were not zealots, like in the big cities, because they themselves were less indoctrinated, given our relative isolation from the outside world. Of course, that doesn't mean that we were generally more tolerant than others, but our intolerance was rather limited to the neighbours from nearby villages, who had been our main enemies for centuries, being the typical rivalries between neighbours. I bet the Führer would have arranged for every household to have a radio, if he had needed more supporters, but we were an insignificant number of souls in that village, which made our political ignorance pardonable by the rest of the world.

However, we did have a radio at the hospital, which Frieda brought in one day. Frieda was a master of providing stuff that was normally difficult to find in those times, though nobody knew her sources. The radio was put in the main hall, where not only the medical staff, but also the patients, could listen to it. So, I could constantly see how, during the stay in hospital, their interest in the political situation grew, fuelled not only by the news on the radio, but also by the intense conversations they had. There was no more powerful fuel for their growing interest in politics, than the sharing of opinions. People, who were lonely at home, finally had the feeling that they belonged. After vivid talks to each other, they became aware of their common roots, which went beyond their direct blood relationship. There was a strong bond of ancestry and traditions which couldn't be torn apart as easily as killing just one member of the family, because it was the essence of an entire nation itself, which should be carried further like parents carrying their ideals forward via their children.

The only one who didn't seem to be affected by the propaganda was Herr Müller. Herr Müller, "der alte Hase" as he called himself, was very sceptical about what he heard on the radio. "I guess they think that the more they repeat the same thing all the time, the more they will convince us, but they won't convince me! I know from my deceased wife, God rest her soul, what this propaganda is all about. When she wanted something, she had to have it, no matter what, so she did her best to convince me of everything, no matter how irrational it was. She kept repeating what she wanted, every single day, again and again. But certainly not as if it was her personal wish, but rather something that should be done, without question, because of a universal unwritten rule, which everyone else was aware of, except me; as if what she said was simply common sense. When I didn't give her satisfaction, she tried to convince everyone around her that she was right, including my family, so in the end, I was the only one who saw things differently. She always managed to make me doubt myself about whether I was right or not. It is reasonable to think that just one person can't be right, when all the rest say the opposite. And this is exactly what propaganda does: convince a critical mass about something, let's say enough people to start a chain reaction. This chain reaction leads to what we call 'common sense' which we all praise, though common sense has nothing to do with reason or logic, but with what the majority think, and since the majority, since time immemorial, have been neither reasonable, nor logical, we come to this."

Hi sighed as he had needed my approval, although I knew it was just one of his tactics to add more drama to his sayings. Seeing that I had no intention to say something, he continued: "And my wife, the old goat, seemed to know all that before our Führer did, and she used these tactics every time she wanted something from me. She even used to convince my own brothers first about what she wanted, and then she allied with them against me. I've always told my brothers that she started to convince the stupid ones first, before she tried to convince me. But they never seemed to get that." and he laughed, and I laughed with him too, because his laughing was contagious. He winked and invited me to take one of the cakes the nightshift nurse had brought him. The cake was delicious and I envied Herr Müller for his energy to keep flirting with the nurses at his age. But apparently the only woman he was thinking about in that moment was his deceased wife, "the old goat". He talked about her with both wrath and affection. "I think what hurt me the most was that she thought that I would fall for her charades every time, as if I was stupid too. Or maybe those were her own limits, and she didn't understand that I could see beyond her lies. That is probably the reason why I now play my own charades with you here. After fifty years of marriage, people become so alike that they even subconsciously mimic what they otherwise consciously dislike about their partner.

Herr Adler never spoke about politics with any of us, at least not at the hospital. Giving that he was our Chefarzt, he didn't find appropriate to talk about his personal opinions with us. He was one of the most pragmatic men I've ever met in my entire life. He struggled to keep the hospital functioning, despite the scarce resources, and he managed to do this task very well. He was an excellent businessman and I would say he was more interested in managing the hospital than he was in medicine. That didn't bother me at all, since my priorities were exactly the opposite. I couldn't stop thinking that compared to Joseph, at least I had had a chance, even in that lost village, and I should be grateful for it. Joseph's desire to fulfil his destiny, as well as his ambitions, were no doubt greater than mine, and even if absolute fairness had ever existed, I knew deep in my heart that he would have deserved this chance more than me, or anyone else, but there was nothing I could have done about it. I didn't even know what happened to him, if he was still alive, if he had managed to escape, or if he had been sent to a concentration camp. I've never stopped thinking about Joseph.

As he promised to me at the beginning, Herr Adler indeed took care of my career by delegating responsibility of the most difficult cases to me, which helped me to gain valuable medical experience. Nobody knew how long the war would last, but I hoped that after the war was over, whenever that was, I could move back to Berlin with my mother, to further my research, as I had done before.

Given the new political regime, I wouldn't have wanted to be in Berlin at that moment anyway, since there were rumours about a euthanasia programme, whose target was those with incurable genetic diseases or other disabilities. This programme, named Aktion T4 after the end of the war, had been initiated as an economic measure, aiming to save money on those who were useless to society.

Despite all the propaganda and arguments made to justify this programme, I knew that I would never be capable of taking somebody's life, no matter what incurable disease that person had, even when I knew very well, as a doctor, what the prognosis was. As a child, I had once had a nightmare about me and several other people having an incurable disease, which left us in unbearable pain. For all those who had this terrible disease, there was the possibility of being put, together with the other incurables, on a train to Cabo de Roca, Europe's westernmost point, where a ship was waiting for us. This ship was supposed to take us to the middle of the Atlantic Ocean, where it was set to explode, saving us from the imminent, unendurable pain at the end.

In my nightmare, when I reached Spain, I realized that despite knowing what was coming next, I didn't want to die. I wanted to live until the end, despite the suffering, because I didn't want to miss any new experiences I could still have, or give up hope, that maybe there was still the tiniest possibility I had been wrongly diagnosed, or that maybe, my symptoms were different from the expected ones. So, I started to scream that I wanted out and somebody should stop that train. And I shouted and I shouted, but since nobody seemed to hear me, I tried to open the doors and the windows to jump out of the train, but it was impossible. I tried to figure out if it was just a dream or reality, but I couldn't, and I still remember all that suffering when I woke up.

So, I knew for sure that I could never obey those new orders and I understood then what Herr Adler had told me on the first day we met, when he said that in those times hiding in a country hospital, in a lost village, was the best choice.

I knew that many other doctor colleagues didn't share my opinion, including one of my ex-colleagues in Berlin, with whom I still had casual contact. He was my friend Peter. "Look Siegmund," Peter tried to explain it to me, "you were lucky enough to be born with two eyes, two arms and two legs and able to walk, run, swim and do whatever you want, including study medicine. But, what would your life have been like, if you'd been confined to a wheelchair, blind or deaf? People like that bring no economic benefit, in fact, they are an economic burden. Also, what kind of life can they realistically expect? Not to mention the burden for the families who have to take care of these people. That's just a merciful death, after all." Peter had always been a cold and methodical scientist and could always explain things so they sounded so rational.

Despite those arguments, or any other rational, scientific or anthropological ones he could use, I couldn't agree that a human being had the right to take the life of another human being. "Then, what about the war?" continued Peter, "People kill each other every day! How many young healthy men have died up to now in this war, some of them leaving small children at home to go to the Front, others leaving a brilliant future behind them, maybe? Isn't that even worse? And wars have happened since the very beginning of humanity – we didn't invent it!" I wish I could have said to him that killing another person was simply wrong and we didn't need to look for logical arguments or sound reasons to justify why we shouldn't kill, that it was just wrong and nobody should question it. But I knew it was useless to make an argument which wasn't one, since I couldn't find any logical reason to support it. "Gott ist tot", God is dead, so the only supporting point I could have brought in our discussion, was also dead with it. Why shouldn't we kill then? Is there any logical argument to support why we shouldn't kill, if the society decides in particular cases that there would be no sanctions for it? Isn't it a dreadful thought?

The border between good and evil was hazy, because morality had become an option, in the power of every individual, according their own criteria, to create and define, rather than a commandment. So I tried to make the only argument I could think of to Peter. "Look, Peter, what if, for one reason or another, you also become useless to society tomorrow?", I said to him thinking of my own mother, whose dementia had got worse lately, making her totally dependent on me. "Or what would it be like if, tomorrow, someone changed the rules, and instead of people with disabilities, this programme was for old people, or people without any artistic talent, or young German doctors? One never knows…"

"Siegmund, you're such a coward!" Peter laughed at me, "Nobody would kill young German doctors, as society would be killing itself. Even those in the highest positions in the political hierarchy need us to survive. There is no comparison. Your example is absurd and has nothing to do with the reality, whether we are talking about today or tomorrow".

But for me, there wasn't any greater cowardice than taking the life of someone unable to defend themselves. And, I also couldn't agree that whenever society, any society, allows us to harm another human being, we have the absolute right to do it without remorse, just because we won't be judged on it. I couldn't accept the idea that life in its essence was so brutal.

CHAPTER 5

Siegmund's diary - Schleswig-Holstein, 25th of January 1940

It was at the beginning of 1940 when Herr Adler started to regularly invite me to have lunch or dinner with his family at the weekends. To be polite, he also invited my mother, but he didn't insist when I told him that my mother didn't want to socialize because she preferred the tranquillity of home. I never told him the truth about my mother's dementia and whenever he asked me how she was feeling, I just answered that she was doing better, constantly avoiding any help from him. It wasn't that I didn't trust him, but my mother had always been a very proud woman and I'm sure she wouldn't have wanted anyone to see her in that condition, except me.

Herr Adler had four girls and a boy, with the boy being the youngest. I guess the Adlers wanted so much to have a boy in their family that they kept trying until they had one. His name was Hans, like my brother, and he was seven. Their oldest daughter was nineteen and her name was Greta, her younger sisters were seventeen, thirteen and ten and they were all beautiful young ladies, especially Greta. She looked a lot like her mother, who was a beautiful woman herself, despite probably being over forty. Even if she was living in a lost and unpretentious village, Greta had a sort of aristocratic elegance, without any hint of arrogance and a sophisticated refinement. One could quickly see that she had received a good education too, from her impeccable manners and way of speaking.

"Greta is a great pianist and she can also paint pretty well." Herr Adler mentioned to me, and Frau Adler nodded in agreement. "If it weren't for the war, I would have sent her to the École des Beaux-Arts in Paris, but given the circumstances, we all agreed that it was better for her to stay home with us, and even if she can't follow her dreams of becoming a great painter, she can fantasize sometimes and at least she can't complain about having a bad life. Can you, Greta? One should be grateful for what one has". Greta didn't answer, just smiled at me sincerely. Although her eyes seemed to smile too, I could see a discrete irony in her eyes when she heard what her father was saying.

However, Herr Adler was right when he said they had a good life and I was impressed by their wonderful house, which Herr Adler showed to me with great satisfaction. Besides their very refined taste, every piece of furniture seemed to be placed in its best possible spot in the house, which made for a generally harmonious impression. The Adlers also had a tremendous art collection: paintings and statues, some of them of well-known painters, like Klimt and Monet. Even if I had already suspected that Adler must have a lot of money, I still found their wealth impressive, given the modest environment we, the rest of us, lived in outside. The greatest part of their wealth was probably inherited, since both Adlers came from rich aristocratic families, as far as I knew.

The only painting that didn't seem to fit in with the good taste of the rest of the house was a portrait of the Führer, which Herr Adler had placed right in the entrance hall, so that it could be seen perfectly well from the first moment one stepped into the house. I almost felt overwhelmed when, right after coming in the door, I met the well-known, authoritarian look of the Führer, who was holding his head slightly to the left, like the Giaconda with a black moustache, instead of an enigmatic smile.

As if he was reading my thoughts, Herr Adler paternally took my arm and said to me, laughing: "Don't worry, Herr Berg, I'm not an admirer, but I receive visits from SS staff too, sometimes. One should be very careful these days, especially when one wants to keep his position and possessions and has a big family like mine to feed. Not that we are starving, as you can see, but we have always had a good life, my wife and I, and we intend to keep it that way. When such harmless gestures may help, why not?"

He smiled to me with great affection, exactly like the day we'd met. "You're still an idealistic young man, I know, but you'll probably have changed your mind by the time you get to my age and you have your own family. In any case, I would like my daughters to marry idealistic young men like you, especially if they have a great future like you do.", and he laughed loudly with the same sincerity Greta had laughed before. I didn't know if he was hinting that he wanted me to marry one of her daughters, probably Greta, or it was just an innocent joke.

During lunch, he continued to drop such hints, which soon became more than just hints, rather direct suggestions. He first started by praising Greta, who didn't actually need any praising, since it was obvious that she had many qualities, which she already knew herself how to gracefully display. "The only thing I regret though." he said to me seriously, "is that, because of this damned war, a beautiful woman like my daughter can't find someone suitable to start a family with, and we don't know when it'll ever end. A lot of good young men are at the Front fighting right now and I wouldn't like to see her become a widow all of a sudden. She is my little pearl after all, and I would like to see her happy."

"Papa, you embarrass me." said Greta, but she seemed to be amused by the conversation, rather than embarrassed. "What if I find a young adventurous painter and we escape together to Brazil?"

"Where will you find him? In the woods? Well, Herr Berg, my daughter especially likes those expressionists, the "die Brücke" painters, you know, but I keep telling her that they are too old for her." and he looked at her with great affection. "They are my age, for Christ's sake, and married too!" and he laughed. "Not to mention that you would get me into a lot of trouble with the regime too, young lady, since none of them are well thought of. As you can see, Herr Berg, none of their paintings hangs on my walls. You must find a clean man to marry too, mein Schatz! You can't get your papa into trouble".

I remembered reading in the papers a couple of years ago that one of the painters had shot himself after his art was considered 'degenerate' by the regime. "As you can see, Herr Berg, my daughter is as idealistic as you. I love young people and although I don't agree sometimes with their unpractical way of thinking, I must say I find innocence is the only reason we should fight. So tell me, Herr Berg, is there a young lady in your life right now? Or an older one?" he asked cheerfully.

I couldn't say that I was taken by surprise, following his numerous suggestions, but I thought for a moment that I was going to faint, which wasn't helped by the fact that the heating in their house was on full, my stomach was full and I had also drunk too much of their excellent French wine. I didn't know how to answer, though I managed quickly to come to my senses, and I answered frankly "No sir, there is no-one, except my mother".

"Dieter," said Frau Adler, "you embarrass Herr Berg with this conversation, please stop it, he is our guest! You must excuse my husband, Herr Berg. On the other hand, he wouldn't be having this conversation if he didn't hold you in high esteem. He has always praised you and your valuable work at the hospital, and I guess he is just getting carried away now by his sympathy for you and also by the wine, probably".

After lunch, Greta played the piano for us, Bach and Beethoven, and she played with such passion and dexterity, that I can say I had hardly heard a better interpretation in my life up to then. I was also impressed how she could interpret the two different styles with such gracefulness. Playing the piano and painting must have been the only two hobbies this young woman could have had in our small village. It was probably a shame that she couldn't go further with her two great passions, but she didn't have a bad life, after all, and I couldn't really say if she would have really preferred an adventurous, unstable life, as she had claimed earlier in a moment of rebellion. But even if the destiny of this gifted girl, raised in a most fortunate family, was to have become a great pianist or a well-known painter, or get married and have children, I couldn't stop thinking that from her point of view; she was another acorn whose destiny to become an oak-tree would not be fulfilled. And I found that ironic, since she was surrounded by the most fertile land one could possibly dream of. I'm quite sure Greta sought, in her own way, a meaning to life in her glass palace, as we all do.

Greta invited me to see a little glasshouse they had at the back of the house. It was actually her mother's hobby, but it was obvious that the aim of that walk was for the two of us to get to know each other better. I didn't want to refuse and I enjoyed her company, so I gladly accepted. Outside the house it was still very chilly and it was good to take a breath of fresh air. Greta took my arm in a very familiar way, like her father had done before. "May I call you Siegmund, Herr Berg?" she asked as she looked at me with her beautiful blue eyes. "Yes, of course." I agreed gladly. "I hope my papa is not too severe with you at work. With us he can be a little severe sometimes, but that's his way." she said smiling. "He can be severe sometimes, but he's a good man." and then she pressed her lips on my right ear to whisper: "He has even helped Jews to escape". I must say, despite having such a severe father, I found Greta rather uninhibited in her behaviour, at least with me. Maybe it was because her father was my superior and her female intuition knew that this must be intimidating for a young employee.

But more than Greta's behaviour, what really surprised me was the little secret she just shared with me, since I saw Herr Adler as rather more of a passive, SS officer rather than an active undercover agent, who helped Jews to escape. I was so astonished, that I didn't know if I should ask her more, or just pretend that I hadn't heard anything. Since I wasn't exactly very sober and lucid at that moment, I decided it was better not to ask. Then it suddenly crossed my mind that if that was true, I could try to find out from Herr Adler if he knew something about Joseph, which gave me a thrill, just thinking about the possibility of contacting him again. How it would be to see Joseph again? Maybe even to rescue him, if he was in a desperate situation? But after quick deliberation, I reached the conclusion that I should definitely keep my mouth shut, because I couldn't take for granted what Greta had said. We were both young, though Greta was even younger and more inexperienced than me and despite her refinement and education she was still just a child, though one who looked like a beautiful woman. And I wasn't quite sure if what she had said she pretended to be true, or just a way to attract my attention. If she had, for whatever reason, lied, and I said something about Joseph, and Joseph was hidden somewhere, I could put him in danger. Not to mention the fact that a house full of expensive art looked rather like the house of an SS officer.

CHAPTER 6

Siegmund's diary - Schleswig-Holstein, 09th of February, 1940

It was a cold night of February, in 1940, when in the middle of the night someone knocked loudly at our door.

"They have come to take us, I knew it!" cried my mother from her bedroom. "God, please have mercy on my soul! Don't let my enemy become my master, please Lord! I've always been faithful to you, and I trust your judgement, so I leave my destiny in your hands. I saw yesterday how those soldiers took Herr Saft with them, and now they've come to take us, too! I saw them, with their black coats and long elephant trunks. They are like big flies, those evil creatures! They will decapitate us and eat our entrails!"

I climbed the stairs to her bedroom and I tried to calm her: "Mother, please be calm. Nobody has come to take us, probably some neighbour got sick or someone is wounded and they need my help, that's all. So please be quiet! I am going to see who's at the door, please don't make a sound."

I opened the door and the nurse who was on nightshift was on the other side. She was freezing. "Ulrike, come in!" I quickly invited her inside. "What are you doing here in the middle of the night? You're frozen! Shall I make you a cup of hot tea?"

"There's no time!" answered Ulrike. "Herr Adler sent me to bring you to the hospital. There is an emergency. A young patient in a critical state needs to be transported by ambulance immediately to Denmark, and he wants you to accompany him and his father to a hospital in Aabernaa and to check on him during the transport. But, I would appreciate it if you have an extra coat to give me; it's really cold outside! And bring something warm for yourself too."

"Hans, who is there?" asked my mother from upstairs. In her later years my mother called me by my brother's name, Hans, and I didn't know if she just mixed up our names, or she thought I was my older brother. I had got used to it and it didn't bother me.

Anyway, as Ulrike looked at me bemused, I shouted: "It's me, mother, Siegmund. Hans went home earlier."

"I heard a woman's voice. Is that your wife?"

"No, mother, it's a nurse from my hospital. There is an emergency and I have to go."

"Are you married?" asked Ulrike surprised.

"No, Ulrike, my mother is just old and sometimes she mistakes me for my married brother, who was here recently, but who has just gone home."

"Of course, he's married!" cried my mother, whose hearing was still excellent, despite the rest of her body letting her down. "And I'm not old! Little whore…"

"Is she talking to me?" whispered Ulrike, who was the innocent seventeen-year-old daughter of a respectable farmer.

"No, Ulrike, I think she is talking to me. She doesn't like being woken up in the middle of the night, that's all. Let's go."

When I arrived at the hospital, Herr Adler was also there surprisingly, and he looked dishevelled.

"Ah, Herr Berg! I've just operated on this young man for appendicitis, but during the operation he lost a lot of blood. We tried to give him a transfusion, but he reacted very badly. I've talked to a colleague in Denmark, who has used those, what are they called… RH groups? And he knows what can be done for this young man and has agreed to take the case on. But the young man can't be transported without medical supervision. So, that's why I called you. Here is his medical chart, signed by me, and a letter for my colleague, Herr Dalgaard. I know it's not going to be easy what I'm asking you to do, to wake up in the middle of the night to accompany a patient so far away, but it's important. They are important people. I hope it won't take too long to transport him and tomorrow afternoon you'll be home again. Then you can take a rest for a couple of days, you'll deserve it. You hopefully shouldn't have any problems at the border, since the guard in charge is the son of one of my ex-patients, whose life I saved a couple of years ago. He will let you pass the frontier quickly, without any fuss. Besides, you're in an ambulance, transporting someone in an emergency situation, so they shouldn't hold you for too long, if there's no reason to. You have your papers with you, don't you? Just show them at the frontier. Now let me introduce you to the Eichel family." and he invited me to the patient's room.

The young Eichel was a twenty-two-year-old man and he was obviously in a bad physical condition. At first sight, I could see that he was indeed very pale and his breath was quick and shallow, though he seemed conscious. His father, probably fifty-years-old, was dressed in a black suit, which looked a little old, but good quality. He just saluted me, but didn't speak very much. He looked absolutely exhausted too, probably from worrying about his son. I noticed that he and Herr Adler didn't look each other in the eye not even for a moment, suggesting there was tension between them.

Remembering what Greta had told me the other day, I strongly suspected, of course, that they were a Jewish family who were trying to escape to Denmark. In February 1940, Denmark was still not under German occupation, even though some of us expected an invasion any moment. So it didn't seem to be an optimal choice, but it was probably the only one they had, and they'd probably bet everything on it.

The young Eichel was covered by a bed sheet so I couldn't see if he had actually been operated on or not. Checking on him and his operated stomach would have normally been the first thing I would have done, but I felt paralyzed, thinking that I might discover that there was no operation on his stomach. It would have meant that I had put Herr Adler in the desperate position of giving me an awkward explanation and put the two Eichels in extreme danger. As I wanted to help them and had agreed to escort them to Denmark anyway, then the less I knew, the better. If we were caught, nobody was going to believe me when I said I wasn't aware of the true state they were both in, but at least my statement would be more convincing if I said I didn't know, because it was only my suspicion, without any proof. But, of course, not acting like a doctor, as I would normally do under normal circumstances, made me an accomplice from the beginning.

Despite all the risks, I wanted to do it anyway. I felt in that moment that I didn't care if I died, if at least once in my life I could do something courageous for a good cause. It would have been my little contribution to justice in this world, which I was starting to believe in more and more. Actually, it is false to believe that we can't perceive and weigh up what is right and what is wrong. Of course we can! It's only that sometimes we believe that we are entitled to do wrong, belonging to a privileged class, entitled to do anything. Fairness genuinely exists, so just pretending that there are no clear limits between fair and unfair, or that these are obsolete concepts, only allows us to keep acting unfairly. I decided that even if I were supposed to die that night, I would still do it. I would cross the frontier with those two Jews and if we weren't caught and I'd have the occasion to do it again with others, I certainly would. And maybe in this way there was a remote possibility to find and help Joseph and his family, too. Who knows? If I had become a member of the resistance, I could have got more information about the Jews who were hiding somewhere and someone would have known something about Joseph.

Herr Adler seemed rapidly to understand that I had deliberately not examined the patient as I should have and he looked at me with gratitude. It was the first time that I had seen the man, who had always been so self-confident and relaxed, almost in a panic. He was blushing and sweating and, actually, the older Eichel seemed to be more restrained in his behaviour, though it was hard to guess how he felt inside, since he was extremely quiet. Probably, he had nothing more to lose, and that gave him serenity.

Then Frieda appeared. She was holding a perfusion which she attached to the young Eichel. She didn't say a word and I'm sure she knew what was going on; could it be that Frieda was in on the clandestine opposition too? In contrast to Herr Adler, Frieda maintained her famous calm and she was the only one that didn't have an odd expression on her face; like nothing was really happening. I must say I admired her for her absolute calmness in these situations. She made all of us feel like children comparing our nervousness with her serenity.

"Well," she said when she was ready with the perfusion "I think the patient is ready to go." I wanted to ask her if she had extracted blood from him to make him look credibly pale and ill, but it wasn't the moment for that type of question. Nevertheless, before I stepped into the ambulance she grabbed my arm and offered me a packet of cigarettes. "Thanks, Frieda, but I don't smoke." "Well, take them anyway, you may wish to start." she said smiling to me in a somewhat maternal way, and she kissed me on the cheek, a little gesture of intimacy she hadn't made to me before.

CHAPTER 7

Christa's notes - Barcelona, 2005

My family almost never talked about my grandfather. However, ever since I had found some photos of him in a magazine in my grandmother's attic, when I was a little girl, I'd always been curious to know more about his life. He was dressed in a white doctor's gown, while working at the hospital, during the Second World War. There were two other doctors in that picture, presumably colleagues of my grandfather; one of them wore an SS uniform and glasses, the other one seemed to be older than both my grandfather and his SS colleague. Something in how the third man was placed in the foreground of that picture and his self-confident look made me think that he could have been their superior. The text had been cut out, so I didn't know what the article was about. I've looked at that picture hundreds of times trying to imagine what my grandfather was doing, what he was like and who the other two guys in that picture were. I didn't know why the text had been cut out, if there was something my family wanted to hide. Then why they still have kept the picture? But nobody ever gave me a clue, and the only answer I've ever got from them is that they have no idea about that picture, as nobody in my family would have known about the existence of that picture in our house.

Questions about my grandfather's life were constantly ducked. The only thing I knew for sure about him was that he had committed suicide shortly after my father went to university. A clear explanation for the reasons which led him to suicide have never been given to me, but it seemed that, some years after the ending of the war, he was accused of taking part in Aktion T4, allegations which caused him severe depression, although they had never actually been proven. Anyway, these accusations ruined his reputation, and after a couple of years, he had to retire from his work, which it seemed he loved very much.

My grandmother never wanted to talk much about my grandfather, and she didn't seem to be fond of him either. Whenever she talked about him, it was only to remind us (especially my father) that she had to go back to work again, because my grandfather wasn't able to provide them with financial security, as he had done before giving up his work. My struggles to found out more about him, and my curiosity to know my family's history better, especially something about what other children could only have learnt at school, left her cold. So I was very glad when a very old friend and university colleague of my grandfather, Joseph, contacted me and gave me his journal, which my grandfather had sent him a month before he committed suicide.

I met Joseph for the first time in Paris, where I was conducting interviews of several intellectuals from the Jewish community who had survived the Holocaust. It was one of my first jobs as a journalist and I was chosen to do these interviews because I spoke both German and French fluently, my mother being French. I didn't study journalism, but philosophy. My father would have wanted me to do something more practical with my life, but it seems that my French blood wins out when it comes to my personality and personal choices. However, he was right, and after finishing university I couldn't do much with my philosophy degree. So, I did a Master in journalism.

Meeting Joseph was one of those encounters that one never forgets, even if they are just casual and inconsequential in one's life. He didn't say anything to me about knowing my grandfather when we first met, and I had no idea who he was. It didn't occur to me that they had ever met, not even when he mentioned that he had studied medicine in Berlin; I could have calculated that they had been the same age. Moreover, besides the fact that my grandfather had been a doctor and had had to quit his profession, I didn't exactly know any other details about where he had studied or when. When I introduced myself to Joseph, and told him that my name was Christa Berg, he slowly repeated my name and held my hand longer than one normally does with strangers.

I kept noticing during the interview that he was studying me with great interest and seemed to be absorbed in every word I said, which I interpreted back then, in my vanity as a young woman, as romantic interest in me, or at least physical attraction. Men usually showed interest in me, so there wasn't anything unusual about that, except that I remember thinking during the interview that the man in front of me had been through a lot, although it didn't stop him finding himself attracted to me, despite knowing about my German origins, and I found that thought very flattering.

I tried not to let it show in my expression, while I was listening to a sad story, which obviously would have been totally inappropriate in the context. And as if it wasn't already embarrassing enough, it came to mind that his name was Joseph, my name was Christa and it just lacked the Virgin Mary to complete the team. I was still very immature and, I guess, still not prepared for that encounter. I believe that was the reason why he didn't mention anything to me back then about him knowing my grandfather.

Anyway, as the interview continued and I was listening to him, I start feeling a great admiration for the man in front of me. Not only had his academic career been impressive, but he was also very modest and serene and, even though he was in his eighties, he was up-to-date in all his fields. He definitely had a much younger spirit, so I could say that my self-esteem had been boosted even more, thinking that he might be infatuated with me.

Seven years later, I received a short email from him, in which he reminded me that we had met in Paris in 1998, that not only had he known my grandfather, but they had been close friends, and also that he had something which had belonged to my grandfather and wanted to give it to me. He told me that he would be in Barcelona in the following five days for a conference, and would be happy to meet me for a coffee somewhere, if I had time and I would like to.

Again, it crossed my mind that his email, as well as being for the purpose he had declared, must have something to do with some romantic interest in me, otherwise, why he would have bothered to find me? I didn't know where he had got my email address from, or how he knew that I had moved to Barcelona, but, I thought that by asking him those questions, I could put him in an embarrassing position, given that he had probably made a great effort to reach me and I didn't want to make such a big deal of it.

Well, nine years after our first meeting, I still wasn't mature enough to ask the simple questions or to understand that I wasn't the centre of the universe and not everything revolved around me. Or at least, I didn't realise that when someone has a romantic interest in you, they don't wait nine years to contact you again, and if they do contact you, it's probably for reasons other than that. Or, maybe I reminded him of an old flame? All that I knew about his personal life was that he lived in Paris, but the rest of his family lived in the US, and he had a grandson about my age, who lived in California and worked in IT.

So I wrote him back to ask him where he wanted us to meet and, also, if I could suggest somewhere; presumably I knew Barcelona better than him. I was quite eager to meet him again for many reasons. First of all, I realized that he had made quite an impression on me at our first meeting, and I confess, if he had been younger, or I older, I wouldn't have ruled out the fact that I might have had a crush on him, maybe... The idea of meeting him again gave me a thrill. And the possibility of finding out more about my grandfather from him was an unexpected bonus.

I still couldn't believe that it could actually happen. What had been the odds of meeting an acquaintance of my grandfather under those circumstances? Besides all that, it was an excellent opportunity to gather information about the subject of one of the books I was intending to write. Since I had moved to Barcelona I'd been writing articles as a freelancer and I'd also started to write books, a dream I'd had since I was a child. Actually, I'd finished and published only one, which had had only mediocre success, and I still had 3 other novels which are works in progress.

The plot of one of these unfinished books is the story of a young doctor who lived and worked during the Second World War in a small village in Schleswig-Holstein, and who had committed suicide after the war was over, for reasons I still hadn't thought of. The unknown story of my grandfather had always been a source of curiosity for me, stimulating my imagination more than anything else.

Giving that I just have a couple of real facts: his photo as a young doctor and the fact that he committed suicide because of some unsupported accusations, I've imagined about a thousand scenarios about who my grandfather could have been. Sometimes, I thought he might have been an SS officer, who despite not being caught or tracked after the war, deeply regretted his actions and that's the reason why he committed suicide. But the scenario I like most is that he had been involved in the clandestine opposition, as a spy for the Allies, and had been caught by the SS and obliged to work as a spy for the Nazis, against his will, so as not to be executed and to continue taking care of his family. Still, he had continued to work for the Allies as a double agent during the war, offering valuable information which brought it to an end. In this scenario, he hadn't committed suicide, but been brutally murdered by mysterious forces, because he was about to reveal a conspiracy he shouldn't have known about. I knew, in reality, that it was impossible, in those times, to actually survive once you were caught carrying out clandestine activities as part of the resistance. And all those caught by the SS, were convicted and executed. Although I've never really believed in conspiracies, I particularly like this scenario as the plot for my book. Yeah, I like to imagine my grandfather as some sort of Superman, who fought against evil forces, no matter what those evil forces represented, only with the aim that good should prevail in the world; like Clark Kent fought against villains in those superhero comic books.

So I was anxious to meet Joseph, who could perhaps know the real story behind my grandfather's death.

"Could you also recommend a place where we could eat?" he wrote me back on Messenger.

"What do you like to eat?"

"Well, almost anything." and he typed a smiley. "But I think something traditionally Catalan would be good. I like to taste the dishes of where I go."

"I think I have some ideas".

"Good! I've been to Barcelona many times, but I've always ended up in the most touristy of places, where they charge double for sangria and add dishes to your bill you've never actually eaten." and he sent another smiley.

"Actually I was thinking of taking you to a touristy place,", and I typed a smiley too, "but yet still a traditional restaurant".

"That's fine with me".

I found it somewhat unusual that a man of his age would use emoticons and, for sure, I wouldn't have been able to guess the age of the man behind the texts sent on Messenger, if I hadn't known him in person. I thought about his whole life and all he'd been through, and how different things were now compared to back then. I imagine he must have had the impression that he had lived ten lifetimes by then.

We met in Plaza de la Universidad and went together to the restaurant. I noticed that he moved a little more slowly than seven years ago and he dragged his left leg a bit. Otherwise, he had the same vitality as before.

It was a little restaurant, L'Oliva, which was my first choice for our meeting. It was a cosy place with excellent food and I thought it would be a good option. We ordered some cheese, *escalivada* and *pan amb tomaquet* to start with, and some wine too.

"Well, Christa, why did you move to Barcelona?" Joseph asked me.

"I came on a scholarship here and I fell in love with this place. I couldn't see myself living in any other place now. How about you? Why do you live in Paris?"

"Well, you may envy me for it, given that you studied philosophy,", said Joseph cheerfully, "but I met Sartre when he came to Berlin on a stipend in 1933, to study Edmund Husserl's phenomenological philosophy, like you came to Barcelona on your scholarship. It was at the beginning of his career and he wasn't so famous back then, of course. I got to know him through a mutual friend who had the same lectures as Sartre at the Institut Français d'Allemagne. We met several times. His ideas changed my view on life in general, and ultimately, my life. When I saw your grandfather for the last time, before the beginning of the war, I already knew that I wanted to live in France. The fact that I was expelled from university in 1935 actually ended up being something positive in my life. I felt so disappointed by the whole situation, that I had an urge to quit Germany, and luckily that was just a few years before the deportation of the Jews began. This is sometimes an advantage of youth, when one behaves impulsively, and takes decisions without weighing things up too much. A 'gut feeling', if you like. Sometimes it's better to act fast. The world is constantly changing, and things around us don't wait for us to weigh them up before taking decisions. If you're lucky, they don't move that fast, so that your decision is still relevant. But sometimes you've just missed the last train. Many of my family members were deported or killed; my own parents among them. My father didn't believe that a man in his position and with his reputation could be just sent to the concentration camp, till the moment the SS came to pick him up. He just waited patiently for things to go back to normal, even after he was expelled from Charité, where he worked as professor. We even had an argument about it. When I left Germany, we actually stopped talking to each other at all; he was a very proud man. My mother tried to make peace between us, but neither of us wanted to raise the white flag. I couldn't understand his passivity and he couldn't understand my impulsiveness. I also couldn't understand how a proud man like my father, with his excellent reputation and great achievements, just gave up when he was banned from teaching anymore. He just accepted it, like it was the most natural thing in the world. I guess, ironically, he was mesmerized by the propaganda aimed at us. So mesmerized that he started to believe that he hadn't deserved the position he had had at the

University. He actually started to think that he had just been lucky before to be tolerated for so long in a position he actually didn't deserve because he was a Jew. Can you imagine that? In the meantime, I was outraged. I blamed his passivity for my own failure, because in 1935 I still believed that my father had enough influence to change things. I thought he could fight for me to be received back at university. But he didn't do anything. Now I know for sure that he couldn't have done anything, anyway. But back then, I just thought that my brilliant future had been lost because of the passive acceptance of my father and of the other Jews. As they all would have accepted that things were just the way they were, and we had been just tolerated until we suddenly weren't anymore. All the contributions that my father and the others had made to the economy, art and science didn't count for anything, simply vanishing in loud propaganda. So I just wanted to run away to France, where Sartre and other thinkers like him were.

"What did Sartre say to you, which convinced you to make that step?" I asked curiously. "I mean, I'm familiar with his philosophy, but what exactly did he say to you in 1933?"

"Well, he was about to develop some of the ideas, which he later also put in writing, that you are probably familiar with. Basically, that we are free to make choices. That we don't have to play a role just because we've been prepared a lifetime for that role, or because our family and friends see us in that role and are expecting that from us, nor even because society or a regime force us to play it. We have absolute freedom, in any moment in our life, to make a new choice, and of course a change. I guess what influenced me the most was the idea that it wasn't necessary to become a doctor just because I came from a family who were almost all doctors, and that was the tradition I should maintain. Not even the idea that I had started to study medicine, was a tremendously good student and could probably have had a brilliant future as a physician, were reason enough not to give up medicine. I was free. I was free to make *my* own good and bad choices. The decision was mine, nothing was predestined. There weren't actually any arguments against the decision to completely change my life, if I wanted to. And this gave me absolute freedom: the freedom to leave Germany where my family had been living for centuries, to renounce the idea of finishing medicine and do something else. To reinvent myself."

"Sorry for asking you that" I said, after letting him finish what he wanted to say, "but do you think you can talk about absolute freedom, when you took the decision to go to France *after* you had been expelled from university and couldn't study medicine any longer? Wasn't your decision forced by the impossibility of choosing exactly what you wanted to do most with your life? Isn't that just a way of fooling yourself into thinking that we are free to make choices?"

He laughed sincerely "Christa, you are exactly like Siegmund, your grandfather. Maybe I just have the capacity to see and interpret things the way I want to see them, while you and Siegmund are realists and analyse it all logically. I wanted to do medicine, and my entire hopes were crushed when I couldn't do it anymore, but it was because, until that moment, I had just seen myself doing only that. I was trapped in my own image of myself and the image of what was expected of me. I was trapped by the idea of stability and financial security, of a clear future and a good reputation. I was only 'the Jew' with a good education and a brilliant future. I knew that I was seen by others as 'the Jew' on the one hand, and the 'future doctor' with a financial security and reputation on the other hand; somewhat contradictory, as you can see."

I smiled. "But you *are* a Jew! *I* see you as a Jew." I said to him with a clear conscience, knowing that I didn't mean any discrimination with that, since I genuinely don't discriminate against anyone.

"Of course I am. But I am because I know it and I accept it, not because you see me as one; it's not a label. It's like thinking of a man who prefers other men exactly like you were thinking of a man who prefers women, without labelling him as 'being a gay', even when you don't have anything against homosexuality. Nowadays, there are a lot of people in modern society who don't have anything against homosexuals, but they still see them as forming a separate group; the society accepts them, but in the mean time they are perceived as being different from the rest. Tell me, Christa, what do *you* thing about homosexuals?"

"I have a lot of friends that are homosexuals. In Barcelona the attitude towards homosexuality is very open. Actually, we are right now on a street where homosexuals can get to know each other, not necessarily in the biblical sense, you know what I mean?" and I laughed and showed him a multi-coloured sign at the corner of the street, which we could see from the very table we were sitting at.

"I'm sure you have a lot of homosexual friends. But what would you say if your son told you he was homosexual? And, that he wanted to marry another man?"

"I'd definitely accept it! Without a doubt!"

"You see? That is exactly my point. I don't doubt at all that you would, but you've used the term 'accept'. You wouldn't have used the same term if I had asked you 'What would you say if your son wanted to marry a woman?' You wouldn't think about being put in the position 'to accept' something. But subconsciously, based on what other people really think, you believe you are in the position to accept or reject." He took a long breath and continued: "It is just that you and the whole of society see homosexuals as belonging to another group, even if you don't have anything against them. It's not about discrimination, it's about classification. And as long as something is classified or labelled, discrimination is waiting just around the corner."

I looked at him somewhat bemusedly. "May I ask you something? Why do you insist on this? Are *you* homosexual?"

He laughed "Besides being a Jew? No, I'm not. I could've been what you call a 'womanizer', if I hadn't met my wife, with whom I was deeply in love. She died from cancer ten years ago, but as you can see, I still wear my wedding ring on my finger."

"Joseph, why didn't you tell my grandfather that you wanted to go to France, if you already knew the last time you two met? And why didn't you tell me from the beginning that you knew my grandfather, if you knew already that I was his granddaughter?"

"Well Christa, because I wanted to be sure that you'd correctly understand your grandfather and accept who he was, before I tell you anything about him. And maybe then you'll also understand the reason why I've contacted you now, but first let me pay the bill and let's go for a little walk, shall we? I won't stay long in Barcelona and I have other things to do too."

CHAPTER 8

Siegmund's diary - Schleswig-Holstein, August 1935

Throughout the whole summer of 1935, Joseph and I didn't speak about his specific plans for the future; we only talked philosophy. We both actively avoided the subject. We'd always been open and direct with each other, but it was an unusual situation and I thought it would be better to wait until he was ready to talk about his expectations for the future. I tried to figure out what he was thinking and what I would I do if I were in his position. I wanted to suggest that he might emigrate as a solution; I knew that some Jews had applied for visas to the United States. Many of the applications had been rejected, but a young man like Joseph, with his status and wealth would have a good chance of receiving a visa. On the other hand, I knew his family had had a long tradition in Germany, living there for centuries, and they had even changed their names in German-sounding ones. They barely spoke Hebrew and they weren't religious either. They were actually more German than anything else and I'm sure that taking the decision to move somewhere else wouldn't have been an easy one. But it was probably the only chance for Joseph to keep studying medicine and become the great physician he was meant to be. It was very hard for me to accept the idea of not seeing him around anymore, but I knew it was best for him and it would've made him happy. Seeing him suffering, even if he didn't actually admit it openly, made me sad too. Since I came from a modest family, without any connections, I couldn't personally do anything for him. I knew that the summer would be over soon though, a new semester would start again and I would go back to university, while Joseph wouldn't.

It was a sunny afternoon in August when we went swimming together. Joseph was very sporty and he used to swim, play tennis and ride a bicycle, so his body was all muscle. The vitality of his spirit was also reflected in the vitality of his body; to me, he embodied the saying "mens sana in corpore sano". As we'd just finished our second year of anatomy at university, it was almost impossible to stop myself from trying to identify the muscles on his body we'd learnt about. There was a big difference between the flaccid muscles on the old corpses we studied, and Joseph's muscles. I realized that, because I had never met my father and between me and my brother, Hans, there was a big age-gap, and Hans had also left home when I was still a small child, I had never had the chance to study another male body - besides mine and the corpses in anatomy class. I felt an impulse to touch his muscles to see if they were really as hard as they looked, but I restrained myself. I almost panicked, thinking that Joseph could find my impulse weird, and therefore he would start avoiding me in the future.

He seemed to notice my unrestrained curiosity to study his body, but it didn't bother him. "What are you doing?" asked Joseph laughing. "Are you studying my anatomy?" I think I blushed because I found my curiosity somewhat unusual, even though it didn't disturb Joseph.

"Well Joseph, actually I am. I was thinking that your muscle tone has nothing in common with the flaccid muscles of the corpses we study at university. We should study anatomy on living human bodies, at least partially, to understand their movement and how they function."

Joseph laughed again. "At least in this case I could still make a contribution to medicine. I could serve as a learning-tool for those who study medicine." said Joseph cheerfully and he sprang into the sea. Years later, when I learned about the experiments that had been conducted on Jews, I deeply regretted my words, even though my stupid words hadn't been meant like that.

CHAPTER 9

Christa's notes - Barcelona, 2005

We asked for the bill and then Joseph and I decided to take a walk together through the historical centre of Barcelona. We had already spent three hours together, but we actually still had a lot to talk about. He told me that he wanted to visit the Cathedral again, because it was something that he used to do every time he visited Barcelona.

The streets were full of tourists, *'guiris',* as they are called by the locals, (even I called them *'guiris'* myself, now I was living here). The number of tourists in Barcelona fluctuates throughout the year, but there is no time of the year when you won't bump into them on the streets, especially in the centre. Anyway, it has never bothered me that the city is so overpopulated and I actually find it to be one of its charms. I have the impression that I'm on a never-ending holiday, and since I'm working freelance, I organize my own schedule and I can write my articles and my books anywhere, including on the beach, or sitting on a terrace and drinking a coffee or a *clara.*

Joseph seemed to enjoy the crowded city as much as I did. It didn't seem to bother him, even if he had to drag his left leg and sometimes he seemed to get tired.

"So when and how exactly did you leave Germany? I remember you avoided answering this question nine years ago, but I would be glad to know now, if it doesn't bother you to tell me privately."

"And you promise not to publish it?" teased Joseph and continued: "It was right after I spent the last summer in Schleswig-Holstein with your grandfather. I never went back to Berlin, not even to say goodbye to my family. I took a train from Hamburg and went directly to Paris. I decided to completely leave my past behind and redefine myself. Of course, I could do that because at that time I didn't think that it would be something irreversible, and I would never be able to see my family again. From the perspective of what we know nowadays about the deportations that followed Jewish persecution, one sees things differently now, but I imagine that nobody would have ever thought in 1935 about what would actually happen later. Nobody could have clearly predicted the war back then, nor the concentration camps or the Holocaust, at least none of those who were victims. So I didn't think in 1935 that I wouldn't be able to go back at anytime and see my family again. It was clear to me that we would never again have the same status we had had before, but not that my family would be killed. I guess I have to live with these guilty feelings now. Otherwise, I don't regret my decision. If there's something that has really pushed me to move forward in life, it's the desire to demonstrate to myself, and maybe to others, that one is the master of his own destiny - this desire has motivated me even more than my own achievements. I could never accept the idea that one should accept life the way it is, and to be happy with what one has, just because there are other people in the world who would be happy to live a similar life, if they could. Of course, comparing it to the Holocaust, the simple fact that I am still alive and relatively healthy and independent at 88-years-old should be enough to make me happy, and I should be grateful. And I am. But that has never been enough for me. I've always wanted to demonstrate that we are free to define our trajectory in life, even if I've always known that we are not completely free. I've always thought that it might be understandable, from a deeply religious man's point of view, to accept things the way they are, since that someone already has meaning in their life, through God. For the rest of us, this acceptance doesn't make any sense though, except when we accept our cowardice. I've never thought that I should be happy with something just because the majority are. It is said that with age one becomes wiser and accepts things the way they are, but unfortunately that has never happened to me. At my age I still haven't become a wise man." And he laughed. "I guess unconsciously I incorporated Nietzsche into my mind when I was young. I consider myself to be an exceptional human being, even if I don't say it aloud.", and he laughed again, and I understood that he was actually being ironic at that moment. "But we have already talked about that in the interview you did with me."

We had just arrived at the Cathedral and in front of it there were two groups of people dancing *sardanes*. Joseph joined one of the two circles and invited me to join them too. I shook my head to signal "no" and instead I took out my mobile phone and I started to take photos of him. As a journalist, I've met a lot of interesting people, but I found him particularly fascinating. When they finished, he came to me and took up the conversation again, as if he had never interrupted himself. "I've always asked myself if Nietzsche would've had other beliefs, or if he would've changed his ideas, if he had lived longer and become old, or if he hadn't been mentally ill. Nobody knows exactly what he had, but I agree with the theory that he suffered from CADASIL, as once I heard at a conference about how mental illness could have influenced the work of famous people. Some believe that he had syphilis. It's curious how even the greatest minds on earth can be reduced to their biology in the end. All our actions, thoughts and decisions are the consequences of our unique biochemistry and of the combination of certain levels of mediators. One can reduce the human mind to that, and furthermore, the entire knowledge and development of humanity is the result of an interaction between distinct profiles of mediators."

"What is CADASIL? I must say I'm impressed with your medical knowledge, giving that you didn't continue to study medicine. You might have forgotten that I don't know anything about medicine, Joseph. Maybe you've confused me with my grandfather. Do I remind you of him?"

"Actually, you do remind me of Siegmund, Christa, and I mean that. But you can be sure I I'm not confusing you with him. Well, CADASIL is a hereditary neurological disease which goes with migraines, depression, stroke episodes and finally patients develop dementia at a relative young age. Nietzsche was depressed, had had terrible headaches since he was young, had at least two strokes which left him paralyzed and in his final years he also developed dementia. So it could have been CADASIL, but nobody knows for sure and it's just speculation. His father died from a brain ailment, when he was still young, too."

I smiled. "I'm depressed most of the time and I have often had horrible migraines. I hope I won't get dementia and die young! I don't know anyone in my family with dementia, though."

"Well," answered Joseph smiling, "if it is going to happen, then, at least, look on the bright side. Maybe you're a genius, too! Many great minds have suffered from mental illness. Maybe it's a condition of becoming an artist. What we consider to be a 'sound' mind is probably a sterile one. This is definitely an argument against eugenics. How many great minds would have been lost, if the strict rules of eugenics had been applied! But even nowadays so many psychologists still classify people with psychometrics, like they would decide which cow should breed for a better milk." and he laughed. "But tell me, why is a young beautiful woman like you depressed, in such a joyful environment like Barcelona?"

"Actually, I was just saying it. I'm not depressed. I was just a little bit disappointed that a book I published didn't have the success I've expected. I just feel that I am at a certain point in my life when I have achieved less than I would have expected, when I was younger. I am thirty-three years old and I can't say that I've done at least one important thing in my life up to now. No family or a successful career. And I can't even say that at least I have close friends, so someone would really miss me if I died tomorrow, no more than a couple of days after my death…, probably."

Joseph looked at me seriously and grasped my shoulders with his big hands: "That sounds like depression to me. You're still very young to be evaluating your achievements, I think, but I understand you, since I went down the same path at your age. And, actually, I wanted to say to you at the beginning that I read your book and I liked it very much. I think you have talent. But maybe you just need a more interesting plot for your next book. And I wanted to propose that you write a book for me - that's why I contacted you."

"For you? What kind of book? Your biography?"

"No, no", smiled Joseph. "It has nothing to do with me directly. Maybe it has more to do with your grandfather's life, but it's not about his life either."

"Then what would be the book about? And why don't you write it yourself? I think an intellectual man like you could write a lot about so many things and it would be a pity if you didn't write about your own experiences."

"No, Christa. First of all, I'm not talented, and then I don't feel like I should be writing this book. Rather, I think you should. I knew it the first time we met. It is your book."

CHAPTER 10

Siegmund's diary - Schleswig-Holstein, 09th of February 1940

While we were still on the way to Denmark, the young Eichel began to shiver. I took his temperature and he did indeed have a high fever. I immediately understood that I had better give up my scenarios and treat him like the patient he definitely was. I took the blanket away and checked his abdomen and I saw that he really had a fresh scar on it. His abdomen was as hard as a rock and he made a grimace although I had barely touched it. I understood that he had probably peritonitis and for a moment I had the feeling that my head was burning and my breath was becoming shorter, too. How could I have been so irresponsible and stupid? How could I have believed that he was faking, and everything was just a cover for two Jews escaping? I felt miserable for not acting like a responsible doctor and I understood that I was still extremely inexperienced, since I hadn't correctly interpreted his symptoms and I had thought someone could fake them so easily. I gave him some aspirin and another perfusion, and tried to disinfect his abdomen, even though I knew the infection was inside. Since there was still no antibiotic available on the market in 1940, I couldn't do much anyway. A lot of people died because of infections and there were more soldiers who died from infected wounds, than from bullets.

The elder Eichel didn't move and his gaze seemed void. He looked at me like someone who, after a long period of despair, had lost any energy to fight anymore. He looked like he was frozen inside in a state of permanent shock. I tried to speak to him: "Your son is in a very poor condition right now and it could be that he won't make it to Denmark. He might die. I'm sorry."

The old man didn't answer me and he just hid his face in his hands. He remained like that, without looking at me, or his son. It took me a while to realize that he was silently crying. "Herr Eichel, what do you want us to do? Do you want to go on to Denmark, or should we go back to your home and family, so that your son can die at home in peace?" He didn't say anything and the young Eichel sighed. I had the impression that the young Eichel was trying to grasp my hand, even though he didn't have any strength to do it anymore. I could barely feel his pulse. So I had to ask his father again: "Herr Eichel, did you hear me? Do you understand me? What do you want me to do?" He finally put his hands down and said: "Well, if my son dies on the way, just leave us both somewhere on the road. We have no home to go back to. And you won't get into trouble because of us. He's the last thing I have on earth, so without him I don't care what happens to me." "Herr Eichel, then we go to Denmark! Please don't give up hope, I'm asking you to do that for me. If there is the slightest chance your son might survive, it's worth trying. I don't care if I get into trouble, and I'm happy to help you two!"

When we were near the frontier the driver beat on the window that separated us from him to let us know that we were close to the border control. I felt my heart beating tremendously fast and I tried to collect myself and prepare some phrases to answer the questions of the officers. I heard "Halt!" and then someone knocked on our door. I opened it and two officers entered the ambulance. They asked politely for our documents. I gave them mine, including the letter signed by Herr Adler, and the older Eichel gave the documents he had for him and his son. They said to me and to Eichel senior to raise our arms and spread our legs and they checked our pockets. Then one of them, with a big moustache, got close to the young Eichel and checked him too. "What are you doing with him? He's almost dying! What chance does he have to survive?" he asked ironically, as if he knew for sure what it was all about. I didn't know if one of them was the son of Herr Adler's patient, and if so, which one. Or maybe neither of them was, and maybe it was just a trap and we'd be shot. I tried to answer calmly: "He is in very bad condition, but he has still a chance of surviving, if he receives the right treatment in Denmark." "It doesn't look like it to me, but if you say so... you're the doctor! Anyway, I can't let you go further until my superior comes to inspect you and gives you his permission. Orders are orders. My orders are to stop any suspect who tries to cross the borders, and you look suspect to me. I have enough experience to smell fugitives, even if your documents are OK."

My nervousness grew, but I did everything I could to remain calm. "How long are we going to wait? My patient, as you see, is in very poor condition, and if we don't continue on our way to hospital soon, he could die! Please have mercy on him. He is a brave young soldier who fought for our Reich, until he got ill. He had appendicitis and has been operated on. But there have been medical complications, he has lost a lot of blood, and now his physical condition is very poor. Only in Denmark can he get the blood transfusion he needs. I must take him to the hospital right away."

"I'm afraid you have no choice. You can tell me all the stories you want; I am a patient man and can listen all day, but it won't change a thing. I won't get into trouble just because you're in a hurry and your patient could die. I understand your rush, but I don't want to die either. You are doing your duty and I'm doing mine. Can you understand my point of view? Either you wait, or the three of you will be shot. I can't make it any clearer than that." he said firmly. "And the driver too", added the other officer grinning.

"May I at least smoke a cigarette?" I asked and I invited them to have one from my packet, too. They nodded in agreement and took one each. "I'm afraid I don't have a light with me, we were in such a hurry when we left the hospital…" I added.

They gave me a light and they lit their cigarettes too. While I was trying to figure out what I could possibly say to convince them, a tall man in a black uniform, stepped into the ambulance. The other two soldiers saluted him and it was clear he was their superior. . He took our documents and had a quick look at me and old Eichel. He got closer to the patient, lifted his blanket and stared at him for a while, without saying anything. The other two waited respectfully behind him. Their cocky attitude had vanished, as if they were a couple of dogs who had just been beaten by their master. Then their superior suddenly turned around and said: "In Ordnung, sie können weg fahren!" as he stepped out of the ambulance, silently followed by his men. Though, I think I heard the one with moustache mumble: "Orders are orders."

Then one of them slammed the door and shout "Jetzt los!" and the driver started the engine and we continued our trip to Aabernaa.

After that night, I started to feel certain complicity with Frieda; we never talked directly about what had happened, but I got the impression that she felt the same complicity, too. We certainly became closer friends. More than once I wanted to ask her what she knew exactly about the two Eichels, how they had got to know Herr Adler and if the young one really needed an operation or if his appendix had been removed to look more plausible. It was a terrifying thought, but in these terrifying times, anything was possible. I would've also wanted to know how much Herr Adler was involved in the resistance, if he had helped other Jews to escape, and what other activities he was involved in. Frieda knew everything that was going on and I'm sure she knew more than me about the whole story.

But I postponed to ask her something. Instead, we began to talk more about our personal lives and there was a certain intimacy between us when we talked about other colleagues or other people that we both know. I also invited her to the cinema in Kiel several times, which Frieda immediately accepted. It was one of our favourite free-time activities and we opted for romantic comedies, which Frieda was delighted with, given that all the other films were basically propaganda.

Like all art, the film industry suffered in Nazi Germany because of the influence which the regime had on it. Many film directors and actors had emigrated to Europe or the US instead of helping the regime in diffusing Nazi propaganda. One of my favourite film-makers was Fritz Lang, who left first for Paris in 1933 and then emigrated to Hollywood. It is said that he took this decision when Goebbels asked him to become the head of his propaganda film unit.

Anyway, despite the war, or because of it, the film industry was flourishing, since many films were made to entertain the civilian population or soldiers. Besides, our internal production had to make up for the restriction which had been imposed on imported foreign films, especially the American ones. For more effective propaganda it was not enough just to highlight what the regime wanted us to see, but also to hide what we shouldn't know. Little by little a new large scale scene was created for us, giving us the impression that we were living in a paradise like Metropolis, without really knowing what was going on underground.

We took our little escapades to Kiel in Frieda's car, which actually belonged to her husband, as Frieda vaguely explained to me. It was a Volkswagen beetle, which was the most popular car in Germany at the beginning of the 1940s'. Must have been one of the army's cars, actually, but Frieda refused to give me more details and I didn't ask. After all, it wasn't my business. I couldn't drive, but Frieda could. Frieda smoked in the car and since she had given me that cigarette packet, I started to smoke too, making her car fill up with thick smoke. "Tell me, Frieda, is your husband still alive? You never talk about him." "Of course, he's alive!" "Why do you say, 'of course'? Isn't he fighting on the Eastern Front? People die on the front, you know..." "That Schweinepriester is never going to die…"What do you have against him? Why do you hate him so much? What has he done to you?" "We were very young when we got married. I was barely sixteen. He was twenty, and worked in a furniture store in Lübeck, and I just wanted to run away from my family, and I found him so handsome and experienced and he mesmerized me with his stories. But shortly after we had moved in together, I found out that he was a drunkard. I got pregnant the first month we were together and when I told him three months after, that I was expecting -I had never found the right moment before that, because he was drunk all the time- he just told me that I should get rid of it, that he didn't want any commitment at that time. When I told him that it was probably too late to have an abortion, he beat me and told me again that it was not his business, he didn't want a child. I could've died during the abortion, but I survived. The nurse who helped me to get rid of my child, asked me if I wanted to become a nurse too, to earn my own money. So, I decided that maybe I should become a nurse, earn my own money, and just move out. I told him that I wanted us to separate, but he didn't accept it and beat me again. He told me that I should never ask him about separation again, because I belong to him, and he will never let me go. I knew he was serious about that. I knew he would rather kill me, than let me free. I was just one of his belongings. I just had to figure out how to live with him further. Well, after that, we found a way to somehow get along, but I never forgot, nor forgave him. I'm happy that he's at the front right now, and I would definitely feel relived, if he died." "Have you ever thought of running away?" "Again? I ran away from my family and that wasn't a good idea. Running away is not a solution. Something that I've learnt in life up to now is that it's better to stay where you are, and cope with what you've got, because if you run away, the problems will follow you wherever you go, and become even bigger." "Then what about the two Eichels?", I finally asked her. "What about them? You saw with your own eyes their probability of making it. Do you really think the two of them survived, especially the young one, and that they are safe now? I'm very sceptical about it." "I don't know, Frieda. I wish I knew…" and I thought again about Joseph and I wanted to know what had happened to him and if his problems had followed him if he had escaped, like Frieda said.

CHAPTER 11

Siegmund's diary - Schleswig-Holstein, May-June 1940

As confirmation of Frieda's scepticism, Denmark was invaded three weeks later by the German army. It was 9th April, 1940. If the two Eichels hadn't left Denmark by then -which was not very plausible given the very bad physical condition of the son- they had probably been caught in a trap without any possibility of escape. She was right; one can't escape one's destiny, so why even try?

I also understood that if Herr Adler had helped Jews to escape through Denmark before the invasion, this wasn't possible anymore.

The same year, in May, a new doctor came to work with us. He was a young SS officer, about my age probably. The first day he came, Herr Adler invited me into his office to get to know our new colleague and asked me to show him around our hospital and explain to him what the daily routine was. I thought Herr Adler would be disturbed by the presence of an SS officer, given his previous clandestine activity, but it didn't seem to bother him, or at least he knew very well how to hide his resentments. If Frieda always knew how to remain calm in desperate situations, Herr Adler always knew how to disguise his real feelings toward others.

Hermann Wagner, our new colleague, was a quiet fellow and very polite with us all, but otherwise rather distant. I don't remember seeing him smile once and he spoke to us only when it was strictly necessary. He lived in Kiel and came to work in a "beetle" every day. It didn't take me very long to notice that his medical knowledge wasn't very profound and he had a mechanical way of treating patients, as if they were cars that should be fixed. I got the impression that medicine was clearly not his life's passion and after a while I started to wonder why he had come -or had been brought, maybe- to our hospital. Without having any evidence for my suspicions, I had a strong impression that his presence among us wasn't aimed at helping us with the large amount of work we had with our numerous patients, but was probably for another reason, one I still couldn't figure out.

Frieda didn't like him at all, but Herr Adler was very benevolent toward him and I thought it was so nice of him because Hermann was an SS officer and he was just trying to protect his status and his wealth, as he had once told me. We were both invited to Herr Adler's house now. Hermann refused him politely more than once, but in the end he accepted the invitation. It was a sunny afternoon in June, when we gathered at Herr Adler's house for lunch. Anyway, compared with the relaxed atmosphere there used to be on these visits, this time it was rather gloomy, at least in the beginning. All the Adler children were more serious than on other occasions and spoke very formally to us and to each other, as if someone had told them to measure what they said before they opened their mouths. After lunch, Greta played the piano, like always, and after that Herr Adler invited us all into his salon to smoke and have a glass of cognac. Amazingly, Hermann became very talkative and he even tried to make a couple of jokes, which weren't actually either subtle or funny. I noticed that during lunch he hadn't been able to stop looking at Greta and after lunch he timidly tried to make advances to her, but Greta was just polite to him and I almost didn't recognize her as the enthusiastic and rebellious young woman I knew she was.

"So, Herr Wagner, are you married or do you have a special young woman in your life?" Herr Adler asked him cheerfully and it was the most authentic déjà vu moment I had had in my entire life. "Dieter, you embarrass our guest," interrupted Frau Adler, "Herr Wagner, you must excuse my husband for his indiscreetness, but I can say in his defence that he wouldn't have asked you something so personal if he didn't appreciate you and your work very much." I had a quick look at Greta and her gaze hadn't changed, like she was in a trance. I got the impression that I had been transported into an expressionist film and we weren't normal people anymore, but characters in an absurd plot. I panicked for a second thinking how little I knew the Adlers and how little my capacity was to analyse people's character. Earlier, I had wished for Greta's sake that her father had found her a good husband to marry, but at that moment I couldn't believe that Herr Adler had been capable of offering his favourite daughter to a mediocre, passionless SS officer, with a dubious sense of humour.

Frau Adler invited me to the glasshouse to show me the new flowers she had got from the Netherlands, while Greta and her younger sisters were sent to the kitchen to bring us coffee and cakes. When we came back from the glasshouse, Frau Adler went to her daughters, while I decided to re-join Herr Adler and Hermann in the salon. When I got closer to the door, I heard them talking about something to do with Admiral Canaris. Hermann was just saying that Canaris would be sent to a court martial and Herr Adler added that it was the best way to treat traitors, to avoid future sabotage of the regime. I knew that Admiral Wilhelm Canaris had tried to warn Denmark about the imminent German invasion a couple of days before the event, and he had been caught, but nobody knew what would happen to him next. It seemed that

Hermann indeed had access to more secret information than us, as I had already suspected. Could that be why he had been sent to Schleswig-Holstein: for political or military reasons related to the invasion of Denmark? If so, why he was divulging this secret information to Herr Adler?

When I entered the salon, they immediately interrupted the conversation and Herr Adler seemed unpleasantly surprised by my appearance. Hermann's face was expressionless, as always, so that I couldn't say if he had also been disturbed by my presence there.

"Herr Berg, I didn't know you were hiding behind the door!" Herr Adler said to me, and even if his tone was cheerful and friendly, I had the acute impression that he was being ironic somehow, and that his comment was aimed at sharing some complicity between Hermann and himself.

"I wasn't. I hope I didn't interrupt a private conversation." "Private?" and Herr Adler looked at Hermann amused. "Herr Berg, we were talking about a rumour that Admiral Canaris warned Denmark about the invasion. I'm sure you've heard it too." "Well, sir, I'm in contact with very few friends or acquaintances, so I'm afraid this type of information doesn't reach my ears until everybody else has heard about it." "Well now you've heard about it. What is your opinion?" I had a quick look at the 'Monet' which was hanging above their art nouveau style sofa, and I answered him prudently: "I think it was a very risky initiative on his part and much unexpected from a man like Admiral Canaris, if these rumours are indeed real." "Well, there is just one name for these types of people: traitors! And they should be executed!" said Herr Adler firmly and Hermann nodded and then he grinned at me as if he knew very well that I was a traitor too, and it was within his power to send me to a firing squad, if he wished it.

I tried to figure out if someone could have told him about my escapade with the two Eichels. The only ones that knew about them and my part in their escape were Herr Adler, Frieda, Ulrike and the driver. It now seemed that Herr Adler had suddenly become a zealous supporter of the regime, although, after all, he was the one who had been most involved in the whole story and indeed, probably responsible for it, so why would he have had any interest in talking about it, and mentioning me? Besides, we had never talked openly about it. I could have denied that I ever knew about the real aim of that trip and say that I was just accompanying a patient, as my superior had asked me to do. Frieda had an open aversion to Hermann and she was involved in the escape as well. Besides, she had known from the beginning what it had been all about and in spite of that she had taken part in helping us with the Eichels. Ulrike knew very little, and even if she did know something, I was sure that such an innocent young woman wouldn't have betrayed us all. And the driver had consciously taken part too and my guess was that it hadn't been the first time he had done it. So it was probably just my mistake, under pressure of the moment that made me think that Hermann knew something.

Luckily, at that moment Frau Adler invited us to have some coffee and cakes and I felt relieved, since the discussion was tense between us, well, between me and the other two, even if I hadn't had any conflict with either of them before and there wasn't any reason for resentment between us, as far as I knew. While we were drinking our coffee, the two youngest daughters played a duo on the piano while Hans sang in a high-pitched voice. "He sings like an angel!" said Hermann with emphasis. "May I congratulate you, dear hosts, for having such talented children? I'm impressed to hear them all, and Greta is not just a beautiful young woman, but also a virtuoso pianist. Her future husband will be a very lucky man, I'm sure. A high class woman like her could bring up marvellous children, the pride not only of her husband, but also of our Reich! Fräulein Greta, I have two tickets for Tannhäuser in Lübeck two weeks from now. Do you like Wagner? I truly hope you will do me the honour of accepting my invitation." Greta almost panicked, but Herr Adler was delighted with Hermann's proposal. "She loves Wagner, Herr Wagner, all of us do! She would be happy to accompany you, of course! It has been a while since my little pearl has been to the opera, hasn't it, my Schatzi? This is exactly what she needs right now." added Herr Adler contentedly and he continued: "May I ask you, Herr Wagner, if you related to our great composer?" Hermann smiled in his rigid way, so that his smile was more like a grin. "No, Herr Adler, unfortunately not. It would be an honour."

Greta looked into my eyes desperately, as she hoped that I would be her saviour, but I could do nothing to rescue her. She almost begged me with her eyes like I was her last hope. It hurt me that I couldn't do anything and I couldn't explain to her why I couldn't either. I also understood that if she interpreted my passiveness as a rejection, it could drive her directly into Hermann's arms, thinking that the reason for my passivity was that she was not attractive enough and then she would see Hermann as her only option for marriage. A young woman's mind is very fragile when it comes to her own image, at least from what little experience I had had of women. I remembered what she had said to me when we were together in the glasshouse: "Do you know why my papa calls me 'his little pearl' sometimes? Because that is the meaning of my name, 'Greta'. It is the short form of Margarita, which means pearl in Greek. He told me that when I was born he fell in love with his little daughter and said to my mother that I was the most precious thing they had, and that's why they named me Greta. You also have a beautiful name,

Siegmund. My grandmother always told me that our name's meaning can influence our destiny. Do you believe that, Siegmund?" "Honestly, I don't. But maybe they can influence your destiny if you believe they can." "You mean if you act in a certain way, influenced by the idea that your destiny is enclosed in your name's significance, like an encrypted message one that should be deciphered? When it actually hadn't any relevance for your destiny, if you wouldn't believe in it? I'm not naïve, Siegmund, even if I'm just a young woman." "I've never thought you were naïve, Greta, on the contrary. And I find your name beautiful, and its meaning too."

It hurt me to see that Herr Adler was about to give his little pearl to Hermann, just to protect his wealth and his valuable paintings. But I knew he was a ruthless businessman and everything had an exchangeable value to him, even his beloved daughter.

It was very late, that night, when someone knocked on my door again. When I opened the door, Greta was there with a little brown suitcase and presumably all of her jewels on, since she had many necklaces around her neck and rings on almost all of her fingers. It was obvious that she had decided to escape from home. I remembered what Frieda had said to me once, that one can't escape their destiny, so why even try? Frieda had probably done the same as Greta was about to do, only more than ten years ago.

Before I could say something to Greta, she put a finger with three rings on my lips and whispered: "Look, Siegmund, I have known for a while yet that my father wants me to marry Hermann, and he will do anything in his power to see that happen. A while ago he wanted me to marry you, but he finds Hermann a more suitable candidate for marriage, since Hermann is a member of SS. I know it's not nice on my part, but many times I've listened at doors to what my father has said to my mother, and I'm glad I've done so. He thinks Hermann could provide me with a better future than you, and it is the best opportunity for me to get married. But I can't see myself being with Hermann. When I think of it, I get nausea. I don't even want to imagine how it would be, if I truly belonged to him. I simply can't do it! I'm not asking anything more than for you to help me escape. I could be a good wife for you, but I understand if you don't want that. Please help me to escape to Paris at least. Once I'm there, you can come back home, if you want to. I'm just afraid to travel alone."

"But Greta, that's insane! Paris has been under German occupation for a short time now. It wouldn't be very easy for us to travel and I'm sure they wouldn't welcome Germans citizens living, studying or working there right now, as they did before. We are their enemies now. Besides, your father would find you, I'm sure of that! I don't know exactly how much your father has to do with the SS and how much influence he has, but given the paintings your father possesses, I would say your father has more acquaintances in the SS than we both know about. And if I don't go to work tomorrow and in the mean time you've disappeared, don't you think he would realize that my absence has something to do with your escape? How can I just go back to work afterwards, like nothing has happened?"

"So you won't even think about staying with me in Paris and never coming back here?" said Greta sadly, and I understood immediately that even if she had said before that she didn't expect any commitment from me, that she just needed a chaperone to France, she actually hoped that I still might be interested in marrying her and living together in Paris.

I felt so sorry for her that I took her in my arms and said: "Greta, we wouldn't make it, believe me. I'm sure that if your father has already discovered that you've left home and he's looking for you right now. And it's almost morning. Soon he will surely be awake, and your family will see that you aren't at home and also that I'm not at work. The two of us just have a bicycle, but he has a car and could send other people to search for you too. We would be fugitives for two hours before they catch us. You would then be married to Hermann as soon as possible and I would be fired. And even if we did escape, which is impossible, you wouldn't be happy with me, believe me! I would probably be the happiest man in the world marrying you in other circumstances, but I just can't be with you. I'm sorry. There is nothing I can do to change the way the things are. The best thing you can do is to talk with your father and tell him exactly what you told me, that you can't marry Hermann and the idea of marrying him is repulsive to you. I will pray that your father listens to what you have to say, even though I don't believe in God."

"My father won't listen to me, you don't know him like I do. He has no feelings other than his greed for money, and he doesn't understand either, that others could value other things more than wealth. He is convinced that what he is doing is what's best for me. He won't change his mind. And I would be happy with you, why do you think I wouldn't? I've had a crush on you since the first day I saw you!" she said in her direct dizzying style, which had I begun to get used to. "I will be a good wife. Why don't you want to marry me?"

"Greta, please, go home. I won't go anywhere with you. We can't marry. My mother is very sick and I can't leave her alone right now. If you don't go back home on your own, I'll have to take you back to your father myself and that will be worse. Go home before the sun rises and your family is awake."

Greta looked directly into my eyes, and I could detect hate in her eyes at that moment. Her passion wasn't there just for playing the piano or running away to unknown places with men she hardly knew, but also for hate, too. However, I understood her. She had the right to hate me, and most of all, to hate her destiny too.

There was yet another surprise I had to deal with soon after. One night, on one of my nightshifts after finishing my work, I went to my office to get some rest and I found Frieda there. She was waiting for me, smoking in the dark. When I opened the door, I smelled the cigarette smoke first, but then I saw her lying on my bed, half naked. It was actually the upper part of her body she'd left completely uncovered, as if she wasn't sure of a result. I didn't turn on the lights and I remained quiet in the dark, because I didn't know what to say to her.

"Do you want a cigarette?" Frieda asked me in her calm voice, like always, like she had everything under control. Under other circumstances 'What are you doing here, nurse Frieda?' would have been the most appropriate question to ask her, I guess, but it was obvious what she was doing, and on top of that, we were friends, so I didn't want to treat her like a stranger.

"Frieda, it's better you put your clothes on, and after you get dressed, we can talk. Please." I could see her in the dark turning her head in my direction, but she didn't do anything. I glimpsed the silhouette of her enormous breasts in a cloud of smoke, like two mountains in the moonlight covered by thick fog.

"Are you sure, Siegmund? I'm not sure you've got this right. I'm not looking for any relationship or commitment from you, and it won't change anything between us- neither in our personal relationship, nor at work. I'm a married woman, after all. And even if tomorrow I were suddenly free, I don't think I would be looking for a commitment after my particular marital experience. I'm an independent woman and I would prefer to remain so, without getting married again." And she paused. "Or maybe I would get married to a rich man like Herr Adler."

"Herr Adler?!" I asked astonished. "Would you marry a man like Herr Adler, Frieda?"

"Why not? He's rich and he likes art. I like art too. Have you ever seen his paintings?"

"Of course I've seen them! But how do you think he got them? I don't know how exactly, but I suspect he didn't buy them from art dealers!"

"Well, one could say he might have bought them… Remember the two Eichels? They were Jews, but not any kind of Jews. Rich Jews. He promised to help them to escape, if they left him their wealth. He kept them hidden in his basement for eight months before he had the opportunity to send them to Denmark. So he actually 'earned' those paintings and that money from them by risking his life and putting all his efforts into saving their lives. It's one kind of deal, after all. And he has helped other Jews in the same way before. It takes a lot of courage to do that, don't you think? He could have lost everything, including his life, if he had been discovered. He risked everything to help them, because he's a brave man."

"Help, Frieda? Do you call what he did 'help'? Once we both talked about the real chances these people had to escape and reached the conclusion that they wouldn't have made it! He stole from them, that's stealing!"

"Don't raise your voice! Someone could hear us. I think he actually risked a lot to help them, so for that at least he deserved to keep their possessions. When one escapes, one can't carry the burden of possessions with them anyway. This is the best alternative for many of them. And I'm sure many of them are alright now. He left them enough money to travel to a safe place, even the United States for the ones who planned it that way. That's the only thing someone can still take with them, when they are fugitives: money."

I suddenly realized that maybe when I had visited the Adlers, the two Eichels had probably been hiding there, like Frieda said, and I felt a cold sweat all over my body.

"Frieda, what you're saying to me is terrible. I thought I knew you better."

"Well Siegmund, you do know me. I'm the same woman you've always known, I haven't changed. Have you ever asked yourself where I get all my money for stuff, where I get all that fancy stuff I bring to hospital sometimes, like the radio, or the gramophone, for example? I thought you'd already guessed where it came from, but you didn't want to ask me directly. Siegmund, that doesn't change anything between us. These are the times we are living in. I'm not better or worse than others. I'm maybe more pragmatic than you are, that's all. Everyone has gained something from it, in the end. Would it have been better if the Gestapo had confiscated all they had and then sent them to the concentration camps? Try not to see things only in black or white."

And she came to me and started to kiss me. I rejected her without any kind of regret while she was trying to reach into my trousers. She took a step back and looked into my eyes: "Siegmund, I would understand if what I had just told you turned you off, but why haven't I seen you with a woman before? I thought it was just me, but I've never stopped wondering about it. You're an attractive young man, but still single."

I didn't say anything to her. Frieda put her clothes on, and before she left the room she turned around and said: "Don't worry. I won't tell anyone. I imagine you're going through hell keeping your secret in these times. You can talk to me whenever you want. You're still my friend, you know." And she shut the door and I wondered if she would ask me for money to keep my secret.

It was a couple of months later when Herr Adler invited me to his office. He wasn't smiling or as cordial as he had been before, in fact he spoke with in a cold, business-like tone and sometimes avoided looking into my eyes. "Herr Berg, my daughter has told me about her little escapade to your house in the middle of the night and that she tried to convince you to run away with her to Paris. I guess I should be thankful to you that you brought her to her senses, and since then she has agreed to marry Herr Wagner, I mean Hermann. They are going to get married two months from now, and we have decided together that she won't say anything about her crush on you to Hermann, nor about her attempt to convince you to run away together. She's still a foolish young girl with a lot of silly love stories in her head. She must have thought she was Juliette and you were her Romeo. She can be very dramatic sometimes, but she's a smart woman. Anyway, I'm not sure Hermann would understand that; he's a proud man. So this is the last time we're going to talk about this subject. I don't want to hear about it ever again. But that is not the reason I wanted to talk to you, though." He stood up and looked out the window. "I was a young man like you once. I know that my daughter is a beautiful young woman, like her mother was, still is. I've always liked women, my wife and others." And he coughed as if he was clearing his throat. "I don't know why you don't like women and it's not my business. I appreciate you as a doctor and more than that, I need staff at this hospital right now. I can't afford to lose people. But I don't want any trouble either. I'm a pragmatic man. So I'll make you a deal, one not open to negotiation. I want you to get married as soon as possible and start your own family, or I will have to report you to the authorities. You know very well what I mean. I don't want to talk about that anymore either. Don't come to me with any arguments, I don't want to hear them. Now, this meeting is over."

CHAPTER 12

Christa's notes - Barcelona, 2007

"So, Christa, when did you decide that you would like to be remembered for eternity?" Joseph asked me after we visited the Cathedral.

"What do you mean by that? Do you mean because I have written a book? The only book I published wasn't successful. At least consciously, I don't think that is the reason why I'm writing. Not to mention that, when someone writes, they take the risk of being criticized, as has happened with me. In my opinion, the only reason one should write is when one feels that they have something to say. If you'll be remembered or not depends on if what you are writing speaks or not to the reader. I've probably failed to do that. To become a successful and well known writer is a long process. It's not as easy as it looks like, before you start writing. I guess the majority of the writers remain unknown."

"Like an acorn which never becomes an oak-tree?"

"Yes, I think this would be the best comparison. The vast majority of the acorns never become oak-trees."

"But don't tell me you haven't ever dreamt about being famous. Every writer is looking to be a celebrity, at least that's what I think. Would you have written something if you were the only survivor of a cataclysm, without any hope of being discovered by aliens who could read what you have written?"

I laughed, thinking about Joseph watching the latest Sci-Fi films at his age. At the same time, I realized how my mind was full of stereotypes, that even I, sometimes, wasn't aware of.

He continued: "It's a human necessity to leave something behind, before we die: children, a house, memories in someone's mind, charity, great achievements, art, etc. Normally good things, of course, but sometimes, what some people consider to be great achievements, means hurting or killing other people, like dictators do. In the end, it's just the desire we all have, to leave a trace of us after we disappear. It makes it easier to accept our death and gives meaning to our existence. Most of us aren't afraid of dying, but rather, we're afraid of being forgotten after our death."

"Do you often think about your death, Joseph?"

"You mean, because I'm old?" I laughed.

"No, Joseph, because you're wise."

"Well, probably no more than you do. I think we have defence mechanisms that protect us from becoming obsessed with the idea, as we grow older. Otherwise, we would be unbearable. I've seen young people more terrified of death than old people. And I don't think our acceptance comes from our wisdom, but because our mind is programmed to give up when there is nothing left to fight for. That's probably the reason why people with terminal illnesses accept their fate at the end. We imagine that the suffering should be worse, but it isn't. You give up only when you know there's nothing more you can do to change things. At that moment, you give up easily or without remorse and my theory is that we are biologically programmed to do that, though it's just my own opinion, since I've never scientifically proved it."

"Have you ever regretted not finishing your medical studies?"

"No, I haven't, though it took me a long time to get used to the idea. Even if I went to Paris, already decided to redefine myself, it took me years to fully embrace my new profession." "Why did you change profession, though? You could still have followed medicine with your recommendation from Professor Reichmann, as you told me in the interview."

"Well, I guess my destiny has been changed a lot by the people I've met in my life, especially when I was young. If Sartre had brought me to Paris, Professor Dumas from Salpêtrière would have influenced me to become a psychologist. He was a psychiatrist in Salpêtrière and he was just implementing psychology as a new discipline at the medical university in Paris. He was supposed to help me, as Professor Reichmann had kindly asked him to, by registering me at the University and helping me to find a place to stay. Though, probably nobody would have guessed that my contact with him would change my trajectory. Actually, it wasn't such a big change from what my work was supposed to be, since I still worked with people. Psychology and medicine are related, but what counted was the novelty of a new domain for understanding the human mind that was just about to be cooked and I had the great honour of being in the kitchen."

"One can see by the way you tell things that you're a psychologist, Joseph. You talk sometimes like you're teaching me. Other times I feel that you're analysing me and what I've said, beyond what a friend would normally do."

"And one can see that you're a journalist." laughed Joseph. "You ask me questions like you're interviewing me. So, I understand that you consider me your friend?"

"Yes. Do you want to be my friend, Joseph?"

"I'd be delighted. And as a little gift to celebrate our friendship, I'm going to give you your grandfather's diary. I imagine you must be very curious to read it."

"Are you also going to tell me what you would like the book to be about?"

"No, Christa, not yet. I don't want to play games with you, but I would prefer it, if you read the diary first and had your own opinion about it. If I told you something about the book, I might influence you, and I don't want that. When you finish reading it, we'll talk again and we'll decide on the best plot together."

"Are you going to try to analyse me based on what I understand of my own grandfather's diary?"

"No, Christa, I'm not an obsessive psychologist. I'm not playing games with you, believe me." laughed Joseph. "Actually, it was my wife's idea before she died. She wanted you to have your grandfather's diary and to write this book for your grandfather, for her and for the rest of us, but most of all for your grandfather, I suppose. You might find some things about him, that you weren't aware of, and maybe some of them will disturb you."

"Why is it so important for me to have my own opinion about the diary in order to write the book? You said that it isn't about my grandfather's life, anyway."

"Well, because, without saying any more, the book is about how someone's opinion, good or bad, can influence other's people minds and make them biased when it comes to a certain topic. It's like planting a seed. I don't want to start by influencing you first."

"And do you expect me to write a book without influencing anybody? That's impossible, Joseph, I don't know how to do that!"

"At least just try to write what you think, without trying to persuade your readers to think in just one way; your way. Give them different options and let them choose for themselves." "I'm afraid that's impossible. No-one can have antagonist opinions about something at the same time. We can't be ambivalent, and whoever says they're ambivalent about something, is either lying, empty. You know that probably better than me. I can only write my own version. But I will read the diary first, and then I'll see what I can do."

"That sounds good."

"Tell me, Joseph, you mentioned your wife, and said that it was her idea. Is that your wife, Greta Adler, the one who started the Greta Adler Foundation, which helped Jews to reunite after the Holocaust and tried to give them back at least a part of their possessions, where possible? I was contacted by the foundation for an interview seven years ago."

"Yes, Christa, she was indeed my wife."

"Was she a Jew, too? How did the two of you meet, if you escaped to France so early?"

"No, she wasn't a Jew. She was German. And it's a long story. I'll tell you the next time we meet. Let's say that both of us wanted to live in Paris, and we met there. Sorry for leaving you with so many unanswered questions. I have to do that."

"May I ask you just one more? Why didn't she bear your family name, though? It is the first time I realised she might be your wife. I hadn't made the connection before, because you two have different surnames. Actually in Spain, it's normal for a woman to keep her surnames after getting married, but not in the rest of Europe."

"When I asked her to marry me, she accepted gladly. She told me that she was an old-fashioned girl, and wanted to get married, but she wanted to keep her family name to remind us that it had been her choice to marry me. And I was happy that she freely chose me. There's no other greater happiness in the world than to be chosen unconditionally by someone."

"It sounds like a beautiful story."

CHAPTER 13

Siegmund's diary -Schleswig-Holstein, 1940-1941,

In the days after Herr Adler had given me his ultimatum, I felt a tremendous sadness for the first time in my life. It was like my entire world had broken down, and not only because I had to take (or not take) the decision to get married, in order to conceal my genuine sexuality, but because at twenty-five-years-old I realized I didn't understand the world at all. I felt completely unprotected. When someone has something to hide, but understands how things work, at least they manage to find ways to protect themselves. But I didn't have the slightest idea about the world, and that was something I had discovered in just a couple of months, so hadn't even had time to learn how to cope with the new situation.

For the next few weeks I went to work like I was in a trance. I just did my job automatically, trying to communicate as little as possible with others, patients and colleagues, and especially avoiding meeting Frieda. Somehow, I managed not to meet Hermann, which was a good thing. I don't think he actively avoided me, and I don't think he knew anything about my whole story either, otherwise I'm sure he would have reported me without remorse. If Herr Adler was just pragmatic and sometimes took contradictory decisions just to keep his position and wealth intact, Hermann seemed to do everything out of a deep conviction. He would have reported me immediately, even if that would have implied losing one or both of his legs. But I guess he was busy with other stuff.

Frieda tried more than once to bump into me, but I politely said to her that I was very busy, and I didn't have time to talk. We only actually spoke when patients were around, just because it was necessary to talk about our work. One day, after work, she came after me and insisted to talk to me. I tried to go faster, ignoring her calling me, but she just yelled louder and louder and I had to stop. I turned around: "What do you want, Frieda?" "To talk to you." "About what?"

"About nothing specifically. I just want to talk to you. Why are you avoiding me?"

"Why?! Frieda, I have a thousand reasons not to talk to you, and you know them very well."

"Actually, I don't. I don't know any reason why we can't talk. Must be only your reasons, not mine, because I'm not aware of any."

I didn't reply anything to her and the only reason I didn't go away it was because I was afraid she might start yelling again. "Siegmund, you need friends. And I like you. I really like you and I know you. How many people you do really actually know? Are you going to avoid everyone for the rest of your life? Let me drive you home. Or would you like to take a walk?"

"Frieda, I'm better alone. I don't need friends. I don't know what I'm going to do next and, sincerely, I don't want to think about it either."

"Siegmund, what did you talk about with Herr Adler, a few weeks ago? I know he called for you into his office. You must have heard by now that his daughter, Greta, is going to marry Hermann…poor child. I imagine what she must be feeling right now. Before, I thought she was just a spoiled young woman, and I envied her for the opportunities she had available to her, but I don't envy her anymore."

"Don't you think she's getting married because she wants to, after all?"

"I don't! But she doesn't have any other choice. A rich and educated woman like Greta seems to have a lot of options, good options, but she doesn't. She must marry Hermann because it's her destiny to marry him. What is your destiny, Siegmund? We all have one. And you know mine, because I was sincere with you and I told you. Well?"

I don't know why I decided to confess to her. "Well, Frieda, ironically, I should get married to. At least that is what Herr Adler told me to do, without giving me the opportunity to negotiate. Those were his words. Did you ever tell him anything about me, Frieda?" I asked her calmly.

"No, Siegmund, I didn't, and I hope you believe that! I would have never done such a thing to you. He must have guessed. Honestly, more than once the nurses and others have asked amongst themselves why you don't have a girlfriend. For a man of your age, they find it unusual. Many have even tried to seduce you, without any success." smiled Frieda. "And we all know that Herr Adler wanted you to meet Greta, a while ago, and maybe also marry her. Refusing the opportunity to marry a girl like Greta, who could be considered by many men as a good match, not to mention she is the daughter of your superior, looks pretty unusual too, even if everyone have their own tastes, of course. For a short while, I thought that you weren't interested in marrying her, because you liked me. Silly, isn't it? I'm still a silly girl, Siegmund, as you see. At least, let's remain friends. Honestly, I promise to behave. I promise I won't bite you!" she said smiling, and I laughed.

It was the first time for a long while that I laughed. Frieda took my arm: "So, tell me, who you would marry? I would marry you, but I'm already married!"

"How could I get married? I can't do that. I'm not saying it because of me, I'm saying it for the sake of the woman I would marry. I couldn't offer her anything as a husband, beyond a stable life, perhaps."

"What about marrying a pregnant girl? A girl whose boyfriend doesn't want to marry her, or having their child? There are many of them! You would do her good. You have no idea how many young girls commit suicide because of it, not to mention that nowadays the abortion has become out of law." added Frieda with her pragmatic way of seeing life.

I looked at her puzzled: "Don't you think that those girls would still want to have a real relationship with a loving husband someday?"

Frieda looked deeply into my eyes: "Siegmund, who would marry a pregnant woman, or a single mother? One can easily guess that you live in your own world, and you have no idea how things work around here. Who knows? What you're saying could make sense in the future, maybe. There are so many widowed women (and there are going to be more) with this war, that maybe it won't be so unusual someday to be raised by a single mother, independently of how that child has come into this world. Maybe the mentality will change. But for now, it is how it is." said Frieda and her cheerfulness suddenly disappeared. She slowly turned her head and looked in a different direction, to conceal her tears. I guess she remembered when she had had to do the abortion herself. "You know, Siegmund, people talk a lot. They have talked about me. They have talked about you too. You can't change them. Even if you try to go unnoticed, as you have been doing in the last few weeks, it doesn't mean they will stop talking. I would say they will talk even more and they won't quit until they find out what you are hiding. But if you listen to my idea, I'll tell you a little secret. Don't worry, I don't normally tell secrets, but this is a secret I'm allowed to tell you."

"That being?"

"Our little Ulrike is pregnant. Can you believe that? Who would have thought? Her father was always very strict. Her boyfriend is a jerk and he doesn't want to know anything about the child, but she doesn't want to give up her baby. She came to me crying the other day and asked me for help. She's desperate. You might be a good husband for her. You would provide a good life for both her and her child and nobody would ask any more questions about either of you. Don't prejudge it! At least, think about it."

CHAPTER 14

Siegmund's diary - Schleswig-Holstein, June 1941

My marriage with Ulrike was, as expected, nothing to be envious about. It wasn't the physical part that was lacking between us, just that we were mentally incompatible. She was a good woman though and she tried to make efforts at the beginning to have a normal relationship with me. I think she also felt grateful to me because I had married her, even if I should have been also been grateful to her. But in reality, our marriage was more like a deal to me. I liked her goodness and her innocence despite what others said about her, as well as her courage in keeping her child, and the sacrifice she made to marry me, just to offer her child a respectable future. But that was all. Maybe the only thing we had in common was that we had both been orphans. Ulrike's mother had died when she was nine and she had been raised by her father. She had three other siblings and was the oldest. She helped her father to raise her siblings and she substituted her mother in the other chores too. She knew a lot about working the fields, the harvest, how to keep a house impeccably clean and most of all, how to raise a child. I guess she couldn't give up her child, because when she got pregnant, her maternal feelings, which had been there for a long time, came out. She didn't take it as an accident, like other women in her situation normally did, but instead, she already saw her unborn child growing inside of her. She wasn't just pregnant, she was bearing a child. It wasn't about her.

From my point of you, since I had been raised without my biological father, I decided to give her child the best future I could possible give. By a tortuous and painful twist of fate, I finally discovered my destiny, as Frieda had said. It was my only chance to become a father. At least I had a meaningful reason to go to work every day, since all my dreams I had had as a student of having a brilliant future in medicine were, under the circumstances, impossible to fulfil anymore. And as Joseph once told me, as I also felt that I didn't have the energy to fight anymore, his theory was that it was probably all over.

Herr Müller kept coming to us, but seldom. One could see that he had lost his previous vitality. It seemed that from his point of view, I had lost mine too. "Herr Doktor, you've changed. What have you done with the obstinate young doctor I knew? I imagine you can't say either... Well, I expected it might be coming. But maybe it was just too soon in your case. I'm sorry."

"Why are you sorry, Herr Müller?"

"I'm sorry every time I see a young spirit dying. You still have a lot of years to live here on earth, but your spirit is already dead. Sorry, but as you see, I've become old and depressed. Instead of making people laughing, as I used to do, now I depress them. I'm a selfish old man. I should be wiser. People expect old people to be serene and give good advice, but I don't know how. I'm not even interested in Nurse Frieda anymore. How is she?"

"Frieda is as you knew her. I don't get the impression that Frieda has changed since I've known her. Maybe she had changed before we first met, so I can't say." "That's what's wrong with you young people nowadays. You get old faster. Where is mankind going?"

It was at that time when I started to notice that all the sick children that came to us for consultation were seen, at least in the beginning, by Hermann. It must have been a decision that Herr Adler had taken; anyway, he didn't discuss his decisions with us, at least not with me. It was probably something that he and Hermann had agreed. After Greta married Hermann, Herr Adler started to call Hermann by his surname again, to keep a professional atmosphere at work, and whenever a child came to us, he said quickly "Herr Wagner, you will be in charge of checking on this child." And then he made no further comments. In time, not only were the ill ones examined by Hermann, but also all the newborns, too. Our child, Arthur, was also to be examined by him, even though we registered his birth in Kiel- Herr Adler told me immediately after Ulrike gave birth. Both Ulrike and I were bemused about this decision. Since I was a doctor too, we didn't see any reason why Arthur should have been examined by Hermann. So I decided to ask Herr Adler why our child should be examined by another doctor, when he was healthy and we, as his parents, didn't see any reason why he should be checked. "Don't you know?" asked me Herr Adler. "It's according to new legislation, that's all. All newborns have to be checked by a doctor."

"But I'm a doctor too. It's not necessary. Arthur is a healthy child!" "It doesn't matter if your child is healthy or not. I just said why; this is the new legislation and Herr Wagner is authorized for that. Even if you're a doctor too, only Herr Wagner can sign the certificate, including Arthur's certificate. You have no authorization. There is no use opposing it, there is nothing you can do about. Arthur must be checked by Herr Wagner and that's it. There are no exceptions to this rule. If he's healthy, there is nothing you should be worried about."

"Why should we be worried?" I asked, and at that moment I understood what the legislation was about. I used to think of it as the "unnatural selection". The social program which aim was to reduce the suffering of the affected ones and save our economy through racial hygiene.

Herr Adler started to write something, as if he was saying to me not to bother him with any more questions, but seeing that I was still there, waiting for his answer, he mumbled without raising his gaze: "I don't know, all parents are worried about their children sometimes, aren't they?"

Later at home, Ulrike asked me what this check on Arthur was all about, and I told her. I saw how she became pale and searched for a chair to sit down. "Siegmund, I'm scared! I don't want to lose my child, I'd do anything to keep him!" and she started to cry.

"Ulrike, there is nothing to be worried about, we are not going to lose him. Arthur is a healthy child. It will be only a check. Don't worry about it. I love Arthur very much too, we won't lose him."

"But I don't trust Hermann. I don't trust him at all! He dislikes you, and officially you are Arthur's father. Don't you think he could write a false certificate, saying that he's ill, just to hurt us? It is completely within his power. You couldn't do anything about it if he did that. He's the only one authorized to examine children and to write certificates. Your word isn't worth anything against his. Don't you think we should run away from here with Arthur? I don't know where, but please, Siegmund, please! We have enough savings to survive until we find new jobs. I don't want to lose my child!"

"Ulrike, look, I know Hermann. He's mean, ruthless and inflexible, but he likes to think of himself as correct. He wouldn't write a false certificate."

"What if he does? I trust you Siegmund, but you can't know for sure. And even if there is the slightest possibility of it happening, I don't want to take the risk. What are we going to do?"

"Ulrike, wherever we go, it will be the same. This legislation is not just here, but in the whole Reich. So, it wouldn't do any good. Trust me, Arthur is healthy and Hermann will not write a false certificate."

"What about not registering Arthur's birth in Kiel?" "Ulrike, everybody here knows Arthur has been born, including Herr Adler and Hermann. We can't hide him."

At that moment, Arthur started to cry. Ulrike wept and said: "He must be hungry. I must feed him." but I saw she was still undecided about ending the discussion: "Siegmund, please promise me we won't let them take Arthur away from us!"

I looked into her eyes and I said her calmly: "Ulrike, I promise you they won't! You can trust me." Although, if Hermann said that Arthur was ill, I had already decided to threaten Herr Adler to report him to the authorities for helping Jews to escape, so that he would felt forced to convince Hermann to leave us in peace. Nobody would care that what he had done was only the consequence of his greed, and that he wasn't actually an opponent of the state. What he had done was against the law. And even if I was accused and put on trial with him, I couldn't have cared less. If they took Arthur away from us, I wouldn't have any reason to live. On the contrary, Herr Adler had everything to lose: his reputation, his position, his wealth and his family. If I was going to Hell, I had decided to take him with me.

A week later, I was going to Kiel to register Arthur's birth. During Ulrike's pregnancy we had bought ourselves a car because it was faster to get home after work. While I was driving into Kiel I thought I saw Greta. I opened the window and called to her, but she didn't hear me or she didn't want to answer me. I tried to park the car somewhere and go after her on foot, but after a short time I lost her. Anyway, I'm sure the woman I saw was her. After eight months of marriage she looked completely changed. She was still a beautiful woman, but she looked ten years older than the last time I saw her. Nothing had changed in her physical appearance, but still she looked very different to me. It was as if she had become more mature in that time. Maybe her clothes and her new haircut gave me the impression that she looked different. It crossed my mind that she now looked like an SS officer's wife, because to me they all looked more or less alike, as if they wore a uniform too; an SS officer's wife's uniform. I wondered if she was pregnant with Hermann's child, though she seemed as slim as always. It was clear that Hermann expected children from her and I thought that after eight months of marriage it would be unusual if she wasn't. Maybe she was. I'm sure Herr Adler would have been delighted to become a grandfather. There were rumours that he was trying to marry off one of Greta's sister too; the next one in line. Even if it was not my business I wanted to know how she was. I suppose I felt responsible for her, in a way. I just hoped that beyond looking like an SS officer's wife, she hadn't been contaminated with Hermann's doctrine too.

CHAPTER 15

Christa's notes - Barcelona, 2007

"Joseph, are you awake? I see that you're still active on Messenger..."

"Christa, it's two o'clock in the morning, why aren't you asleep? I'm an old man and four hours of sleep per night are enough for me; I couldn't sleep more even if I wanted to. But you should be sleeping. Why are you awake?"

"I've been reading the diary, I mean not all of it, just the first pages. I have to ask you something, otherwise I just won't be able to sleep. I hope you'll answer me and stop putting off answering my questions. There are important things about me and my family here. What's the point of keeping me waiting?"

"I think there are important things you might learn from the diary and you should be prepared for them first. I think of you as a very dear younger friend, or even as if you were my own granddaughter. That's why I've taken time with you. But if you want, I can answer your questions directly. So tell me, what do you want to know at two o'clock in the night?"

"From what I've read, I understand your wife knew my grandfather and she even wanted to marry him when she was young? And you knew that? I mean you read my grandfather's diary too, didn't you? So the fact that we met wasn't just a coincidence? Our first interview is something that you and your wife had planned together?"

"To answer your last question, yes, my wife and I had planned to meet you and give you your grandfather's diary. We both kept in contact with Siegmund after the war. We knew that he had a son, your father, Arthur. Siegmund asked us to look after him when your father decided to study in Paris. He just said to Arthur that we were some old friends and gave him our address in Paris. We met your father a couple of times, but he was too busy courting your mother, so he didn't pay us much attention. Actually, the last time we saw them both together, was when your mother was pregnant with you. We invited them to a party with some artist acquaintances of my wife; a type of event we thought a young couple might also enjoy. But after your birth we lost contact. We would call Arthur sometimes by telephone to ask if he was okay or to see if they needed something. Siegmund loved your father very much; we knew that when you were born too. After thinking about it for a long time, we decided you should have Siegmund's diary. We thought it would be easier for you if we met and talked first. Are you still awake?"

"Yes, Joseph, of course! How could I go back to sleep after all the new things I just learnt from you?!"

"How much have you read until now?"

"Up to the part where your wife knew my grandfather. I confess I was shocked. I wanted to talk to you. I know it's late. I'm sorry. I just wanted to talk to someone. I have the impression right now that my family and I are the characters in a novel, whilst I always thought that my life was boring. Suddenly it's all so exciting! Everyone knows everyone, like the characters in a detective novel, where the murderer finds out too late that the victim was actually his own brother! Or like in one of those soap operas. Do you want me to write a soap opera, Joseph? Nobody would ever believe this story is actually real. I don't even know myself what to believe. I didn't know anything about you until nine years ago, and even though it seems now that you've met the most important members of my family, none of them has ever said anything to me about you and your wife. Then, you give me a diary that could belong to anyone, or to be written by yourself and you expect me to believe these stories, just because *you* tell me they're real. Why should I take for granted what you're telling me? Why should I believe you?"

"Well, the story is real, Christa, but you can believe it or not; that's your choice. Apart from Siegmund's diary, I don't have other evidence to support what I'm saying, unfortunately. You see? I'm talking about evidence, as if I should prove something to you. Sometimes people believe things that aren't real, and sometimes they don't believe what is real. I can do nothing else to prove to you that this story is real. I'm not asking you to believe anything either. I guess you could search in archives for the names of the people that appear in the diary and to find out if they were related to your grandfather and if the facts are real. You're a journalist, it's part of your job. But it might be that a part of the information has been lost to time. We normally reach conclusions based on the evidence we see, but we miss the fact that there are many things we don't actually see, even if they did exist. We can only be in a certain place at a certain moment and that's the reality we perceive and take as 'the real thing'. Maybe we would have a different perspective if we could be simultaneously in different places at the same time, or in the same place at different moments. But it's physical impossible. Our perception is limited, but we reach conclusions based on that narrow perspective and we take it as reality."

"If I decide to write a book based on my grandfather's diary, could I change some facts and characters, even some of the historical events, or should I keep to the real story?"

"You can change whatever you want: facts, characters, names... It's your book, write it as you wish, in your own way. Don't expect people to believe the facts you describe in it, that's not the idea. It's just a reflection on how you interpret this story. It's fiction, not science. And even science is biased, in my opinion."

"Then what should we take as reality? There must be one that we all perceive in the same way, otherwise we couldn't interact with each other. Whether correct or not, our perception should be the same."

"Should it? I bet we have the impression that we are talking about the same thing right now, but we have different perspectives. Which one is correct? Mine or yours? Each one has their own reality. Cogito ergo sum. Look at mentally ill people. They have a totally different perception than ours, just because their brains are set up differently. They see and hear things we don't perceive, and don't perceive other things that we see and hear. The majority of us are set up in the same way, which we consider to be the 'correct' setting. But is our perception real, or complete? Maybe if, in addition, we had other types of neurons, with different functions than the ones we already have, we would be able to perceive and understand other things too. We don't know that. Our biological limitations define how we perceive the world."

"Well, maybe you don't exist, Joseph. Maybe I just invented you. Maybe you're just an illusion that my mind has created."

"Maybe. It's a possibility. Now get some rest. Good night!"

"Joseph, may I ask you one last question? Please…"

"Ok, but that will be the last one for tonight. After that, I am going to shut down my laptop."

"How did your wife get to Paris in the end?"

"As an SS General's wife she could cross frontiers without any difficulties. Hermann was a general by then.

She just said she was going to meet her husband in Paris, where he was waiting for her."

"And instead of him she met you?"

"Good night!"

CHAPTER 16

Siegmund's diary - Schleswig-Holstein, 1941, 15th of August

As I expected, there were no problems with Arthur's certificate. He was as healthy as I already knew he was, and Hermann wrote what he found without taking advantage of his position to hurt us.

Since Hermann had been promoted to General, he had become very benevolent with the rest of us, and even more open and talkative. He behaved like a normal human being, let's say. Sometimes he came up with some brilliant ideas, such as exchanging the women's pavilion with the men's one because there were more beds in the men's and we had more female patients; an idea that Herr Adler found magnificent, so in the days that followed he couldn't stop praising Hermann for his brightness. After such smart contributions, we all had to hear Herr Adler eulogizing Hermann's ingenuity and his capacity for understanding the complexity of hospital management. However, despite not having personal problems with Hermann, I didn't feel comfortable at all knowing what his new duty of examining all the new-borns consisted of. I wasn't involved in it, but I was aware of it, and I did nothing, even though I could guess what happened to those children Hermann found physically or mentally disabled. I was there, I knew about it, but I didn't do anything. What could

I have done, anyway? It wasn't just Hermann, it was the whole system. Hermann was just one of the marionettes, a rat who was convinced that he was doing what he was supposed to do, but who wasn't the root of the evil. I couldn't denounce him as it wouldn't have made sense, since he had been put into that position by his superiors. It wouldn't have done any good even if I had killed him, though the thought had crossed my mind more than once. But I knew he would have been replaced immediately by some other 'Hermann' anyway, and it would have just meant disaster for our family. Convincing him or even begging him to write false certificates concluding that the disabled children were healthy in order to save some of them, was useless. I knew he wouldn't listen and he didn't care. The only thing that crossed my mind was to talk to Greta. I knew Hermann loved her very much in his own way. I don't know if Hermann knew what real love was, but at least he was infatuated with her. Maybe Greta would be the only human being he would listen to. But I didn't know how I could reach her, how I could talk alone with her for a short while, and even if she would want to listen to me. After getting married, she had moved to Kiel and once in a while she came to visit her family, but I wasn't welcome in her family's house anymore. Although I didn't have any conflicts with Hermann, we weren't close to each other and he didn't invite us to his house, not even once. I knew that they went to the opera regularly, so it would have been possible to meet her there, although I couldn't be sure that I could talk to her in private. Besides that, I didn't usually go to the opera and my presence there might look even more suspect to Hermann, since he knew I had a small child and Ulrike to take care of at home. I had to figure out another way to meet her.

Then I remembered that on my way home sometimes I saw Greta's little brother, Hans, playing with other children. One day I took a wooden airplane toy that Herr

Saft had made for me when I was a child and when I saw Hans again, I called to him. He remembered me and immediately came to me with a big smile on his face.

"Guten Tag, Herr Berg." he greeted me. "It has been a while since you have come to our house, Herr Berg. Is it because my older sister Greta got married?" he asked me seriously in his childlike innocence.

"No, Hans, it's not because of that, it's because I got married too and I have a little boy at home. His name is Arthur. I have to take care of him. How are you, Hans?"

"I'm fine, thank you. I miss the old days. It's a little boring at home right now"

I smiled to hear to hear how he was trying to talk like an adult to me. I took the wooden airplane and I gave it to him. "Hans, look what I found the other day at home. It was my toy when I was your age, and I used to play with it all day. I even took it to school. I used to imagine I was a brave pilot who fought in the Great War, rescuing my father from death. Would you like to have it?"

"Don't you want to give it to your son, when he grows older?" Hans asked me and I appreciated his maturity and lack of egoism.

"Well, Hans, we could make a deal. I could loan it to you for a while, and when my boy is a little older, you could give it back to him and teach him how to fly it. What do you think? This airplane is only for brave soldiers. Are you a brave soldier, Hans?"

He smiled and I could see how the child inside him was coming to the surface. He took the airplane and did some circles with it in the air. "Hans, do you know what a secret agent is?"

He looked at me somchow offended: "Of course, I know!"

"Would you like to become one?" he nodded with interest. "Do you promise to keep the secret just between us? You have to swear to me, Hans."

"I swear!"

"Are you sure you want to do this, Hans? Because it might be dangerous…"

"I'm not afraid of anything, Herr Berg. I'm a brave soldier!"

"That is what I wanted to hear. And you can call me Siegmund, if you like."

"What am I supposed to do, Siegmund?"

"Well, your first mission is to give your sister Greta a note from me. But the most important thing is that nobody must know anything about it. Nobody! None of your other sisters, neither your parents, nor Hermann. Do you think you can do that?"

"Of course I can! That's easy! Is Greta a spy too?"

"Soldier, you know I can't divulge the identity of our collaborators. I can't answer your question, I'm afraid."

"What is in the note?" "Well, that's a part of your job you might not like. You can't know what is in the note either. Normally, secret agents don't know the information they are carrying. Do you know why? Because if they are caught and tortured, they can't disclose any information, simply because they don't know anything. It's logical, isn't it? We must be sure that the enemy, under any circumstances, won't get the information."

"But I wouldn't say anything, even if I were tortured. I'm a brave soldier!"

"Have you ever been tortured, Hans?"

"No, I haven't."

"Then you don't know that for sure, do you?"

"No, I don't." admitted Hans.

"Ok, then I'll give you the note for Greta and you give it directly to her without reading it and without anyone else knowing anything about it. Is that clear, soldier?"

"Clear."

"Do you know what to do, in case you're caught by the enemy?"

"Don't tell anyone, anything, sir?"

"That's right. But besides that, you have to swallow the note."

"To swallow the note, sir?"

"Yes, Hans. To eat it. That way, the enemy won't come into possession of our top secret information, will they?"

"That makes sense."

"Most of all, you must be sure Hermann doesn't know anything about it. He's the bad guy in our story."

Hans looked at me puzzled. "Siegmund, do you really think Hermann tortures people?"

"Why do you say that, Hans?"

"You said that if I get caught by Hermann, he'll torture me, and that's why I should swallow the note."

"That is not exactly what I said, Hans, but if I were you, I wouldn't take any risks. So, before I give you the note, let's repeat it, one last time. What you are supposed to do, soldier?"

"I am supposed to give Greta your note, without anyone else being aware of it, especially Hermann, sir!"

"Very good, soldier! And what should you do if you get caught?"

"Eat the note, sir."

I searched in my pocket and I took out the note that I had prepared at home for Greta. It was just a little piece of paper where I asked her when and where we could meet, and I had signed it, Siegmund. I didn't tell her the reason why, in case Hermann came into possession of my note. It was better he thought that I was infatuated with his wife, which probably would have been his first thought, than knowing the real reason I wanted to talk to her. It wouldn't have put Greta in an odd situation, since he had probably thought I was just a lunatic obsessed with his wife.

"Agent Hans," I said to Hans before saying goodbye to him, "I will contact you again to see if Greta has an answer for me. Just be in the same place after she gives you her note to me."

In the next few weeks, I waited to see if Hans had an answer from Greta, but I didn't see him. My anxiety grew when I no longer saw him around and I wondered what had happened. Had he given the note to Greta? Had he talked to someone else about it besides Greta, and he wasn't allowed to see me anymore? Had he been caught when he tried to give the note to his sister? Or had he just swallowed it before he had even seen her? Where was that little schlaumeier? It was already autumn, the days were shorter, the wind blew the whole day and it rained often, so the chances of seeing him again became fewer. I just hoped that he had at least given my note to Greta, and even if he didn't appear again until spring, maybe she would try to contact me in one way or another.

Meanwhile, my life alternated between home and the hospital. The only true happiness in my life was Arthur, who had become the main reason I woke up every morning, hoping that one day I would understand through his eyes what meaning my life had. Like all parents, I was truly convinced that his life would be better than mine and he would fulfil all his dreams -or actually, all the dreams that I was unable to fulfil for myself. I guess that is the trick life uses, in order to convince us to procreate, or in my case to raise a child that wasn't even my blood; the perpetual hope that the next generation will do better than we did, a trap into which every parent falls. In this way, life goes on, while every single one of us dies. The intelligent design of life, a concept Joseph was so excited about. He always believed that life, independent of the order we are all struggling to make of it ourselves, has its own organized structure, and everything around us can't be just the result of random incidents. "There would have to be way too many random causalities." Joseph used to say, every time he wanted to make his point. He didn't see his personal failures, or what we generally consider to be negatives in this world, like wars, death, crimes or injustice, as a counter argument for the existence of an organized framework. Instead, he thought that we had to understand why the negative events should also exist. "Have you ever had a nightmare, Siegmund? I mean I'm sure you've had one, but do you remember any of them?" "Why do you ask, Joseph?" "Well, do you know that sensation, during the nightmare, when you are truly convinced it's actually real? And then you wake up, and realize it was just a dream, and nothing you convinced yourself was real, actually happened?" "What is your point, Joseph? Because I can't follow you, I'm afraid." "Well, what would it be like, if we had the same perception of what is happening around us right now? One day, we might wake up in a different reality, and we would understand that what we are living right now was just a dream? Even if for us it was the only reality we had been aware of. Wouldn't all the negative things, that are happening, be less important then? Or not important at all? All that happens in a nightmare doesn't count once we're awake." "Well, even if it was as you say, Joseph, although it's just a hypothesis you can't support, how would this change the life you are aware of, right now? And I still don't understand what your point is." "It probably wouldn't change my life, as you suggest. But it would change my perception about life in general, because we consider life to be imperfect based on the meaningless bad things which inherently happen, but maybe we would consider it to be perfect, if we could find a meaning for those things, when seen from a different perspective." "I think minimalizing what we judge as being bad could be dangerous, Joseph. It would imply that doing bad doesn't actually do harm, as long as we could understand its meaning, if you see it from your perspective. After all, this is the only reality we are aware of, and there are no hints of the existence of a different reality as you suggest. What is the point in hypothesizing about something we have absolute no evidence exists? If someone you care about were struck by lightning tomorrow, would you suffer less if you could find the reason why that had happened?"

But Joseph was keen on this theory and never gave up trying to convince me that he was right. In his opinion, understanding this intelligent structure would help us to find personal happiness, therefore this should be the meaning of our life; simply to understand. Because it would be easier for us to accept, and even to overcome our pain, if we had a purpose at the end of it, or if we could know why things are supposed to be as they are. Even the bad things. It's just a matter of understanding. "Call it God, Nature, or Universe, this is actually what every scientist, theologian or philosopher tries, in their own way, to comprehend; everyone only concentrating on their tiny field of research. We only take small steps in our short life and they're not enough to allow us to see the whole picture. We only see fragments of it and understand only what our mind and senses allow us to. What would it be like if we actually knew how this big machinery works?"

Herr Müller had the same philosophy as Joseph. Herr Müller had never finished school and probably hadn't read a book in his whole life, but, as he liked to say about himself, he was a wise old man, someone who had gone through life questioning everything. We always had something to talk about. I didn't think, in the beginning, how much I would be pleased to see him every time he came back to us again. He liked to find an explanation for everything and I enjoyed hearing his new speculations. He also read me like an open book. "Well, Herr Doktor, what are you going to do now?"

"What do you mean, Herr Müller?"

"I mean medicine is not what it was before, is it? Before, it was supposed to cure people, but now it is supposed to select the healthy ones, and kill the rest. Isn't that irony? I can't see a warm heart like yours fitting into this picture anymore. Luckily, you're not directly involved in it, like Wagner is."

"How do you know about these things, Herr Müller? I barely know about them myself. You aren't supposed to know about them."

"Na ja. An old man always has his sources. If I told you that I've talked to God, I would be the next one on that blacklist, wouldn't I? So, I'd better keep quiet."

"Do you talk to God, Herr Müller?" I asked almost stupefied. It was the first time I had heard him saying things like that, and I was afraid he might have developed schizophrenia, although he was a bit old for that.

"No, my son, I don't. It's just a way of talking. When someone is old, they can read the minds of others, especially an old goat like me. I can read your mind. Haven't you noticed? I read your mind the first day I met you. I've read your heart too. You won't kill me for that, will you?"

I laughed. "No, Herr Müller, I won't kill you. But if you keep talking like that, I might give you some pills to swallow."

I left him in his room, playing cards on his own (or with God, who knows?), and I went to see other patients. When I left his room, it occurred to me that I still hadn't received an answer from Greta or little Hans.

CHAPTER 17

Siegmund's diary - Schleswig-Holstein, 15th of September 1941

It was about that time, when to our modest provincial hospital the family von Hülsen came for the first time for a private consultation with Herr Adler. Admiral von Hülsen was a descendant of the Prussian Chief of the Königsberger Land Regiment, and it was more than unusual that they chose to come to us, whatever their medical problem was. Their noteworthy appearance was even more remarkable because they came to us with all their seven children, all wearing elegant clothes, as if they were coming to a dinner party. Their fancy clothes and refined manners were unusual at the hospital. The family had two sets of twins, one pair were identical little girls, whilst the other twins were a six-year-old girl and boy. The little boy was brought in in a wheelchair, and at first sight, I suspected that he might have hypoxic-ischemic encephalopathy, a neurologic disease caused by a lack of oxygen during birth. However, his twin sister seemed to be fit and healthy and was walking side-by-side with her little brother's wheelchair, holding his hand. Sometimes, she whispered something in his ear and he laughed, which their parents didn't seem to like, because they turned round and said "Shhh, shhh!", reminding their children that they were in a hospital, and had to be quiet.

I was having my morning coffee, when Frieda came into my office to bring me our new patient files. "Do you want me to open the window? This room needs a little fresh air. And you too, Herr Doktor." she said, while she tried to organize the mess I had on my desk. She threw away a couple of old biscuits that were lying there, without asking me, and took away the empty cup of coffee from yesterday. Then, uninvited, she sat on one of the two chairs I had on the other side of my desk. It was clear she wanted to stay a little longer for a chat, as she usually did, from time to time. She lit herself a cigarette. "Do you want one too?" I shook my head to show that I didn't. "That little boy, Werner, one of the children of the family von Hülsen, is supposed to be our patient. He's the twin of that sweet curly haired little girl who always plays around his wheelchair and whispers little jokes to him. She's a sweetie." She took one of the patient files she had brought, and gave it to me. "I read it this morning. I was curious to know why they'd come to us. The little boy has hypoxic-ischemic encephalopathy, after birth asphyxia. He was the second one out, and the labour was hard and long. It seems that since birth he's been paralyzed and retarded and he also has epilepsy. Hermann wrote in his file that apparently the boy has been very agitated lately and even aggressive toward his siblings and the family considers it would be better if they separated him from the rest. They say he has had a mental breakdown and that's why he needs fresh air, and peace, and quiet. That's why they came here to this remote village, instead of going to one of the university hospitals in Berlin."

She looked directly into my eyes as she was expecting me to say something, but we both remained quiet, looking at each other. I knew what she was trying to suggest to me, but I had nothing to say. I didn't know anything about the boy, or his family. After a pause, seeing that I didn't intend to make a comment, she changed the subject: "How are you doing? How is little Arthur?"

"He's growing up. He's crawling."

Frieda sighed. "You know, Siegmund, I've never been sure if I want to have children or not. When I was pregnant, I was very happy at the beginning and I wanted to become a mother. It was probably my maternal instinct triggered by the pregnancy. But right now, I don't know. I don't think I know how I should raise a child. I mean not the day-to-day care, of course, but what I should teach them about life. You see the world we are living in. I wouldn't want my child to be like Hermann one day, but I couldn't raise them to be against the system either. As a mother, my first worry would be their wellbeing, which implies their adaptation to this society too, and only after I was sure they had accomplished that, would I care if they were also moral human beings. Isn't that what all parents do?" and she smiled. "How are you and Ulrike raising little Arthur?"

"Without thinking too deeply about it, like you're doing. I guess when one has a child, you don't have time to ask yourself too many philosophical questions. You just raise them, on instinct, as you say. The first priority is their survival. Of course, I want to be sure that he will receive a good education. But probably because that is related to his future wellbeing, as you've said. Besides that, Ulrike has read a book about raising children, one written by Johanna Haarer. Maybe you've heard of it."

"The book that advises to let your child cry when they need you, just to make them stronger? The one adapted from our Führer's book, 'Mein Kampf'? That is how you and Ulrike are raising Arthur?" she asked stupefied.

"Frieda, personally, I haven't read it. I don't have time. But Ulrike has raised many children before, her siblings, and I'm sure she would never leave Arthur crying." I looked at her, as she was sitting in front of me, with her hands sitting softly on her lap, her mouth still slightly open in stupefaction, and a meek expression on her face. I don't know why it came to mind, that if I had been a painter, and I had wanted to paint the portrait of a mother with her child, or even the portrait of Virgin Mary, this was exactly the expression I would have been looking for. Why? I don't know. Ulrike would probably have been a more suitable model. "You should have a child, Frieda. You would be a good mother."

She looked at me resignedly. "I don't know, Siegmund. I'm not sure I want to have one. I have a good life, at least it's the best I've ever had. For the first time in my life I feel I don't belong to anyone, but me. Before my husband went to the Front, I always belonged to someone. I had the impression that the real me was locked inside my mind, whilst the one others wanted to have around, was living my day-to-day life. It's difficult to explain. Now it's different. I know you don't agree with my lifestyle, but it's the one that suits me best. Maybe you think that I'm irresponsible, or selfish, because I don't want to have children, as a woman is supposed to have, but I'm OK with that. I'm happy with myself. I don't hurt anyone. I leave everyone else in peace. And the only thing I ask for, in exchange, is also to be left in peace. That's all."

"I've never said I didn't agree with your lifestyle, Frieda. And about having a family, who am I to judge you? You made me marry Ulrike, remember? But now I'm very happy with my family. I love Arthur. He's a blessing. He's the best thing to have happened in my life, thanks to you."

Frieda laughed. She seemed to be proud of herself because she had done a good deed. I continued: "I just said you'd be a good mother. That is what I think. You care about people, and as far as I know you from work, you're practical and responsible. Maybe you remind me of my own mother, that's why I make the association."

Frieda laughed again. "So you think your mother raised you well? Do you think you are a good example for other women to have children because of the way your mother raised you?"

"Well, what do you think? Did she raise me well?"

She deliberately didn't answer my question to tease me, as she did sometimes, to tease me, but added: "How is she, your mother?"

"She's not very well. Her health is very poor, I mean she's a lot worse. Ulrike is an angel. She takes care of my mother when I'm not home. My mother is more work for her, than Arthur is. She's like a seventy-kilo baby, with an ugly personality. She's completely lost in her own world and totally dependent on us. But she has kept her strong will, which doesn't make it easy for us to take care of her. Ulrike is a very good woman. She has a lot of patience, which I don't have. As I said, she's an angel. I'm lucky to have married her. But under no circumstances would I judge you for not having your own children, Frieda. Everyone is different. Ulrike is meant to take care of her family and she gave up her hospital life very easily. I don't think she would like to come back here and work as a nurse. For her, it was a necessity to work as a nurse to feed her other siblings, not a choice."

"Well, Siegmund, you probably don't judge me, but I know a lot of people do. Especially the other women-colleagues. Even when I don't hear them, I know they are talking behind my back."

"You shouldn't care. I know it's not easy, but you simply shouldn't. The fact that your husband is never home, gives you a good reason not to have any children, doesn't it? If you had a child right now, they would say you'd cheated on him. Let them talk. Even if you had children, they would invent another reason to talk about you. They envy you. They will never stop finding a reason to tease you."

At that moment, the secretary knocked on my door and stepped in. She said that Herr Adler wanted to see me. "Is the file of Werner von Hülsen with you? Herr Adler said to bring it with you, when you come."

"I have to get back to work." said Frieda.

"Take care of yourself and your family. And tell me what the matter with that little boy, Werner, is. I'm curious to know why they have come to us instead of going to a bigger hospital in Berlin. Something smells fishy to me with this fancy family. I don't know why, but I'm afraid of the worst."

She was about to leave the room, when she turned around, "Thanks for talking to me. It did me good. I'm glad we stayed friends."

CHAPTER 18

Christa's notes - Barcelona, 2007

"Well, Joseph, have you read any of what I sent to you of my novel yet? I haven't heard anything from you in the last few weeks. I'm curious to know your opinion. And I'd also like to invite you to an electro-swing concert in Barcelona in two weeks' time, if you want to come."

"Sorry Christa! I've been very busy and I haven't had time to read what you sent me yet. I've also felt pretty tired lately, so that anything I have to do now requires at least double the amount of time it used to. I guess I've finally got old. As for the concert, Christa, I don't think so. I haven't been to any concerts lately. But I'm planning to come back to Barcelona soon. I want to do at least a part of the Camino de Santiago route, as far as I still feel myself able to. So, first I am going to take a flight to Barcelona, and then probably the train to Ponferrada. I hope you'll do me the pleasure of meeting for coffee. Then we can talk about your novel, too."

"Didn't you like my novel? Isn't how you expected it to be?"

"Christa, I haven't had time to read it. I mean it. You're too impatient."

"Well you're my first reader, Joseph. And the most important! I'm writing this book because you want me to write it. So I assume that if you haven't *made* time to read it and/or you haven't said anything to me yet, it's because either my novel isn't interesting enough, or it's so bad you don't want to say anything because you don't want to hurt my feelings."

"No, Christa, it's because I've only read the first five chapters and I wanted to read it all first, before giving you my opinion. We men are different. Sometimes we leave the more important things at the end, after we first solved the 'unimportant' ones. We have an inverse priority. That's why you women consider us unpractical. In fact, we want to be sure that we've taken enough time to weigh things up properly before we give our opinion."

"Don't you think that you're being a little chauvinistic when you say that? People may think you are saying women don't weigh things up enough, before giving their opinion."

"I didn't say that. And I don't care what people think; I'm too old for that."

"By the way, if they don't know who the writer is, do you think people will be able to guess that this novel is written by a woman, and not a man? Particularly, since the main character is a man and I'm writing from his point of view."

"I can't say. I haven't given it much thought. And, I know very well that you wrote it. So, I guess subconsciously I know it is written by a woman. Is that important to you?"

"No, no. I was just curious. Because sometimes when I was writing it, I was thinking what a man would think in that situation. And sometimes, I had the feeling that I was being too melodramatic, like, for example, the story of the two Eichels. I get the impression that a man would use more violence than melodrama. In the diary you gave me there is too little information, just a couple of thoughts my grandfather wrote down now and then and I had to invent a lot to make a novel of it"

"Now who's being a chauvinist?"

"Why?"

"You've just said that when something is written by men, it implies more violence. Do you think all men are violent?"

"No, Joseph. That is not what I meant. I don't think all men are violent, just their style of writing: Hemingway, Dos Pasos and others. I've never read books written by women with very much violence in them."

"Well, I've never read all the books written by women. But it's true; the ones that I've read aren't violent."

"Besides, I had to select and adapt the medical information Siegmund wrote in his diary. There was too much of it. Sometimes, it gave me the impression that I was reading medical files, not someone's diary. I don't expect people, other than doctors, to have any interest in reading all that stuff. He was clearly passionate about medicine!"

"He was indeed."

"And I had to invent some characters too, like Herr Müller and Frieda. If not, it would've been a novel with only two or three characters talking to each other about medicine, in an ultra-specialized medical language. Well, it might have been possible, but maybe too modern for my style of writing and boring for the large majority of readers. I hope you don't have anything against it."

"Of course I don't. It's your novel. You only can write it in your own style."

"I created Herr Müller inspired by you. Did you recognize yourself in Herr Müller? And I think I see Frieda as my "Doppelgänger". She has my personality; some of the lines she says are things that I've talked about with my friends, or my own thoughts. I'm afraid she is maybe too modern for those times? My grandmother and I didn't have a close relationship, so we didn't talk much. I also lived in France for many years and we didn't have any contact. It's difficult for me to imagine women's mentality in those times. Things have changed a lot in-between, especially women's mentality."

"Well, Christa, you would be surprised to know that people's thoughts and feelings haven't changed that much. What has really changed is the fact that a lot of these thoughts and feelings are brought to the surface, made public thanks to the existence of the media: radio, television, and recently, the internet. The fact that sixty years ago it was scandalous to see two people kissing in a film, doesn't mean people didn't kiss back then."

"I know that, I googled it. I also googled some historical facts and to understand some of the medical terms Siegmund used in his diary."

"Google tells you all you need to know nowadays, doesn't it? Who needs books or libraries anymore?"

"Sometimes, I get the feeling that what I've written is a cliché. There have been so many documentaries, books and artistic films about the Second World War, Nazi propaganda and the concentration camps. But even if I try to avoid a cliché, I still have the feeling that I can't escape my own mind-set. Probably, because I've seen too many films about it. I'm not sure that people will understand that I'm not writing about a specific moment in history, rather about what nationalistic propaganda can do to society in general, independently of the moment in time and the historical context."

"I think art can only reflect the present, even when it talks about the past. It's like a screen-shot of the emotional echo that shadows the historical facts at a certain moment. It doesn't have to reflect the real facts, like history does, but the emotions which emerge from the social, political or economic context. These emotions can embody events from the past, if this makes them easier to rise to the surface. If it sounds like a cliché, it's because life is a cliché and historical events just keep repeating themselves, with different protagonists. By the way, what do you think about this? I've just sent you something by email. Have a look at it and tell me what you think."

What Joseph had sent me was a picture. The picture contained an old letter, which had a yellowish tinge, a coffee stain in one corner and it seemed to have been typed on an/a (old-fashioned/classical typewriter. It was dated 6th June, 1907 and it was addressed to Albert Einstein. The letterhead contained the name of the University of Bern and at the end it was signed by Professor W. H., the Dean of Sciences. There were only two paragraphs communicating to Einstein that his application for a doctorate had not been successful and therefore, he was not eligible for the position of Associate Professor.

"Where did you get this, Joseph? Are you in the possession of the actual letter?"

"No, no. I've never held this letter in my hand. I found it on the internet. Why do you think I would have it?"

"I guess that is the first thing that crossed my mind when you sent it to me. Without thinking too much, you're a Jew and Einstein was a Jew. And you've met famous people like Sartre, so why not Einstein, too? And what other reason could you have to send it to me?"

"Well, it doesn't belong to me. What do you think? Try to imagine writing an article based on this letter, as part of your work as a journalist. Would it be something you think would be worth writing an article about?

"It seems to be a rejection letter addressed to Einstein by the Dean of the University of Bern for his application for the position of Associate Professor. Where did you find it on the internet, Joseph?"

"If you type in 'Einstein's rejection letter', it's easy to find it on different webpages. You can verify if for yourself, if you want."

"Is it one of those motivational posts one can find nowadays on the internet? Probably a lot of people would feel motivated if they knew that the famous Albert Einstein had been rejected before he gained recognition."

"Do you think this letter is the original? Isn't there something unusual about it?"

"I can't say. I don't know too much about Einstein's trajectory in life, so I don't know if this application was real or is just an invention. I can't say if the date is correct, for example, if he was really rejected or not. I would have to google it, I guess. What is your point?"

"You don't have to know any of that information. I think that only with what you know about Einstein, it's enough to decide if this letter is a fake. What do you know about him?"

"He was a physicist. He wrote the theory of relativity. He was a Jew, born in Germany, and he emigrated to the United States when Hitler came to power. When he emigrated he had already developed his theory of relativity and was famous all over the world. He didn't get citizenship for five years, after emigrating to the US. This letter had apparently been sent to him before he emigrated in 1907, when he was probably still young and at the beginning of his career. Wait a moment! I know what you mean. The letter is written in English. And Einstein's mother tongue was German, and the official language in Bern is also German. So, it makes no sense that they would've written a letter to Einstein in English at that time, when English wasn't even the official international language; it was French. Now I understand what you mean. It can't be the original. Although someone probably went to a lot of trouble trying to make it look so.

"Bingo!"

"Well? Why did you send it to me?"

"I found it on the internet the other day, and I thought it was amusing. I wanted to see if I could prank a journalist with fake evidence."

"Well, Joseph, you did prank me! Honestly, I thought it was something related to our story. Let me know if you decide to go to that concert with me. I might surprise you as well."

CHAPTER 19

Siegmund's diary - Schleswig-Holstein, 15th of September 1941

"Frau von Hülsen, may I present our trusted committed young doctor, Herr Berg? He has also worked and did research at Charité, until he joined us, two years ago. He's a dedicated young man, and especially fond of children. He has his own son. Arthur is his name, isn't it? This little young man, Werner, is going to be in very good hands."

I was still standing behind the chair where Frau von Hülsen sat when Herr Adler began to make the introductions. He seemed to be in a good mood so he spoke quickly and cheerfully, as I knew he did whenever he was good-humoured.

I came closer to them, and Frau von Hülsen lifted her head to look at me and raised her right hand in my direction. I bowed and kissed her hand, which was covered by a silky pale-green glove. She discretely bowed her head and smiled to me benevolently.

"I'm glad to hear you come highly recommended, Herr Doktor Berg. You see, in our family we are very close to each other. We raised our children in the Christian family spirit. God knows, when my husband and I aren't be around anymore, our children will take care of each other, as we have taught them to do. I'm relieved to learn that our little Werner is going to be in good hands. Do you mind if I ask how old your son, Arthur, is, Herr Berg?"

"He's eight months old, Frau von Hülsen."

"Oh, still very young, the little fellow. Aren't they adorable, when they are so little? I hope he's healthy, too!"

"He is a very healthy boy."

"Health is the most important thing a parent could wish for their children. Werner is such a lovely boy, you see, so sentimental. I remember when I took him in my arms for the first time, after a long labour. He had such little hands and feet, the smallest I've seen in all my children. I had such a strong desire to protect that little soul. Do you understand what I mean, Herr Berg? I'm sure you felt the same, when you took your own son in your arms for the first time."

The small talk with her made me feel distressed and I didn't feel it was appropriate to talk about Arthur with strangers, either. I hoped she would soon get to her point.

"You see, Werner has been seen by many doctors, but we've never left him alone in a hospital before. We would like to be sure he'll be fine. I'm sure he will be fine in your hands, Herr Doktor." She paused. "I hope you understand how much we love Werner. My other children will miss him at home, especially his twin sister, Elisabeth. We've never been separated before. I wouldn't want him to think that we've just abandoned him here."

"There have been always many children in our hospital. It will be a warm environment for Werner. He will have other children around to play with, if he wishes, and you agree too. It's always good for children to socialize here; it makes their stay in the hospital more pleasant."

"Of course we agree. We have nothing against Werner mingling with other children, but he is a special child. I'm sure all the children here are well-mannered, but I know sometimes children can be very sincere in their behaviour. I don't want anyone to hurt him, even by mistake."

"They won't!", said Herr Adler with emphasis. "Someone from our staff will always be watching him, dear Frau von Hülsen. You can go home assured. Your son will receive the best possible care we can give him."

"Well, then we will stay here for just a couple of days more. Then we will back to Berlin. My husband has important things to do there, and he is going back this very night. We've never stayed separated for too long. We'll come to say 'good bye' to Werner the day after tomorrow. If you need anything from us, you know where we can be found."

"Of course, Frau von Hülsen, I promise you Werner is in very good hands. Herr Berg is an excellent physician and a warm-hearted human being. We will take care of your son and I will personally write to you and your husband to inform you about his progress. This fresh air will probably do him good. You may go back to Berlin in peace."

"Well, thank you both, dear gentlemen. I don't want to waste any more of your precious time. Good bye."

I accompanied Frau von Hülsen to the door and I turned around to see if Herr Adler wanted something else from me, but he was already doing paperwork, so assuming he had nothing more to add, I left too.

Werner was waiting outside in his wheelchair, and his curly haired sister was embracing him, while they touched each other noses. They both laughed to each other. Frau von Hülsen sighed.

"I know that for Elisabeth it will be very hard to be separated from her brother. They are very close. Our other twins are not so close, even if they are identical. That's probably why my other twins are more independent. Neither of them is confined to a wheelchair. But I'm afraid Werner will never be an independent human being. Elisabeth has promised to take care of him her entire life... She's such a sweet child! But her destiny is to get married and have her own children one day, not to take care of her ill brother.", and she sighed again. "From the beginning Elisabeth and Werner have stuck to each other like glue. I've always thought that Elisabeth has wanted to make it up to her brother for being the healthy one. We've never explained to her why her brother is ill. Oh, it was such a long labour. I thought it would never end and I even thought I would die. I must confess I had a couple of moments when I simply hated Werner, for not coming out sooner. But of course that changed when I held him in my arms for the first time. I immediately forgot about everything. And now, look at them both. They're inseparable. I've never been very close to my siblings. Do you have siblings, Herr Berg?", she asked. "I have a brother." "Do you get along with him?" she continued, which I found inappropriate. "He lives in Dresden. That's why we don't see each other often, especially now with the war." "Ah, so…" she murmured and then she turned to her curly haired daughter: "Elisabeth dear, give your brother a goodnight kiss. We have to go now. You are supposed to be in bed soon, and Werner, too!"

She took Elisabeth's hand and pulled her firmly away, while the little girl tried to hold on to her brother's arm. "May I stay here with Werner, Mutti? He will be so lonely here, without us. I'll tell him our goodnight fairy tale. He can't sleep without the fairy tale, Mutti..." "No, Elisabeth, you can't sleep here. This is a hospital, dear; hospitals are only for sick people. I'm sure this nice doctor will tell Werner his goodnight fairy tale. Now, say 'Good bye', darling. It's late for the both of you. You should both be in bed, dear." Elisabeth didn't seem very convinced, but as she probably knew there was no sense fighting anymore with her insistent mother, she turned to me resignedly: "Will you tell my brother a story, sir?"

I was about to reply when I heard Herr Müller's voice behind me: "I will tell him as many stories as he has patience to listen to. I know a lot of stories, little girl. What is your brother's favourite fairy tale?" "Hänsel and Gretel." said Elisabeth shyly. "Do you know that fairy tale, sir?" "Of course I do, little girl. I promise you solemnly that your little brother is going to hear his favourite story tonight, before he goes to sleep. If not, I promise to let myself be eaten by the bad witch. Go to sleep, little girl. I'll take care of your little brother, Fräulein." "Have you heard that, Schatzi? Now give Werner a goodnight kiss. Good bye, Herr Doktor. We'll come again tomorrow." "Good night, Werner. Sleep well. I'll think of you the whole night." promised little Elisabeth and then, after giving me and Herr Müller a shy goodbye wave, she followed her mother out the door.

CHAPTER 20

Joseph's notes -Paris, 1941

Madame Petite was a middle-aged widow, whose body matched her surname perfectly. Despite being rather corpulent, she was also short; so short that she barely reached the shelves in her kitchen to take down the coffee cups always asking me to do it for her, whenever I went over to pay my rent. She was the most talkative woman I've ever met and she talked very fast too, so that even if I understood French very well, after six years of living in France, her *Provençal* accent made it difficult sometimes for me to catch what she was saying. Since I couldn't understand her very often, I stopped asking her to repeat herself. I just drank my coffee nodding whenever I got the impression that she wanted me to agree with her, or smiling neutrally whenever I guessed that she was just telling me one of the stories about her family, or her deceased husband. Her only son had died a year before, fighting against the Germans. So, Madame Petite hated Germans even more than the rest of occupied France, who hadn't lost a close relative to the conflict. That's why I was sure she wouldn't turn me in to the Gestapo, and I knew I was safe with her. She suggested that I say that I was a Belgian from the German-speaking Community of eastern Wallonia, if someone asked where my accent came from. She also offered to iron my shirts and whenever she was cooking one of her famous "daube" or "ratatouille" she used to knock on my door and give me some of her delicious food. She also kept telling me that I should look for a good mademoiselle to start a family with, insisting that, even though she had been a widow for a long time, and she had lost her only son, her family had been the best thing she could have had in life. Since she was like a mother to me, and I didn't know anything about my own mother anyway, I asked her kindly to simply call me 'Joseph'. It seems, though, that her good manners, which she had picked up as a child in a modest working-class family in Marseille, were so deeply engrained in her character, that she could only call me "Monsieur Joseph".

It was a nice summer's day when Madame Petite came to my door with her "ratatouille" and a key to another room in our building that she wanted to rent.

"Monsieur Joseph, my sister passed away yesterday and I have to go to Marseille right away. I will probably stay there a couple of weeks. A nice young lady, Mademoiselle Dubois, is going to rent the room in the attic and she's supposed to come this weekend. I ask you kindly to give her the key to the room and to apologise to her that, given the unexpected death of my sister, I haven't had time to organise the plumber to repair the toilet in her room. I will do my best, when I return, to get it repaired as soon as possible. Tell her that I won't ask for any rent until the toilet is fixed. She can use the toilet downstairs; the one that I have for the guests. Please don't forget to tell her that I won't charge any rent, until she can use her own toilet. She's such a lovely young woman. I don't want to lose a tenant like her."

"Don't worry, Madame Petite, I'll tell her everything you want me to tell her. I can also show her the neighbourhood, in case she's not familiar with it."

"Oh, that would be so lovely, Monsieur Joseph. But please don't try to fool around with her, I know you've broken the hearts of some young -women, but she's such a lovely girl. She doesn't seem to be from here, either."

"Don't worry, Madame Petite, I won't break her heart. Maybe she'll break mine, if you say she's so lovely."

"Oh, Monsieur Joseph, she's very beautiful and well educated, too. I'm sure she would match your taste in women. That's why you should be careful. I just want to warn you, because you'll have a 'coup de foudre' when you see her.", continued Madame Petite with her usual appetite for drama. In saying so, she had piqued my interest in this young woman, when what she really wanted was exactly the contrary.

"Don't worry, Madame Petite. I'm a grown man. I know how to take care of myself. You don't have to worry. You can go in peace to your sister's funeral. I'll just show the girl the neighbourhood and give her some tips about where she can buy groceries and meat, but that's all. Nothing will happen."

"Oh, thank you, Monsieur Joseph, you're so kind. There should be more well-educated young men like you in this world. God bless you, Monsieur Joseph!"

Without anything else to do, after she was gone, I remembered I hadn't been to the *friseur* for a while, and that I might need a couple of new shirts for work. At least I had plans for the next few days, which I was looking forward to, given that I hadn't had any, since I had broken up with Jeanette.

When I came back from the barber's, I found a young lady waiting on a chair at the entrance, with a little brown suitcase at her feet. She was reading a book and didn't seem to notice my presence at first. But when I came closer, casting a large shadow on her book, she raised her head and I could see her beautiful blue eyes inspecting me with curiosity, while she involuntary raised her perfectly shaped eyebrows.

"Mademoiselle Dubois?" I asked her, the tone of my voice a little fainter that I would have liked it to be.

"Oui." And she gave me a big smile. "I'm Hélène Dubois. And Monsieur…?"

"Joseph, you can just call me Joseph."

"Is your surname 'Just', Monsieur?" and she smiled.

"Or are you a spy and you don't want me to know your surname? That's okay; you don't have to divulge it to me, if you don't want to. I appreciate confidentiality myself."

Exactly as Madame Petite had predicted, I was immediately charmed by my new neighbour. However, I couldn't help but notice that Mademoiselle Dubois had, despite speaking excellent French, a discreet German accent. Maybe Madame Petite couldn't identify very well where her accent came from, but I could, and I had no doubts that she had been raised in Germany. Anyway, I didn't know if she was a Jewess, German or another nationality. Her traits, the colour of her eyes and something in her self-confidence told me that she was German, but I didn't know why she was trying to conceal her origins, except perhaps a willingness to please the locals or to integrate more easily into the community. I didn't get the impression that she had run for her life from Germany, because she wasn't trying to remain unnoticed. Anyway, any local would have easily noticed that she had an accent, one which was pretty much the same as that of those who were occupying their beloved city. So, what was the point of giving a French name when the locals can detect that you are not French? Maybe she was a spy. Or maybe she was hiding from the Germans?

"Hélène. That's a wonderful name. I'm sure you could start a war, if we weren't in one already. I mean, the Trojan War. I mean, did your parents think of Helen of Troy when they give you your name? That is what I'm trying to say. It suits you." Usually, I was a pretty confident guy, but at that moment, I felt the more I talked, the more ridiculous I must have looked to her. I blamed Madame Petite and the lobbying she had done for this girl, even before I had met her, for putting me in a vulnerable position, and making me make a fool of myself in front of her.

I was expecting her to take advantage of my vulnerability and to mock me, as sometimes French girls did, but she smiled at me very sincerely and said: "My grandmother always said to me that our names can influence our destiny. Do you believe they do?"

"Maybe they could influence your destiny, if you strongly believe they can. Does that make sense to you?"

"I know what you mean. You remind me of someone, when you say that.", and I detected some nostalgia in her voice.

"An old flame?" I dared ask her.

"I guess you could say that. But it was a long time ago."

I wondered how long ago, because she looked still very young to me. Was she twenty-two, twenty-three? Or maybe twenty-five? But definitely no more than that. It wouldn't have been polite to ask her, though.

"Madame Petite asked me to give you the key to your room. Her sister died the other day and she had to go to Marseille to her funeral. She also asked me to forgive her because your toilet doesn't work, and she didn't have time to get the plumber to fix it."

"Oh!" exclaimed Hélène, obviously distressed.

"Madame Petite said that you don't have to pay her rent until your toilet is fixed."

"It's not that. It's just that I need to go to the toilet, right away."

"You can use mine, if you want."

"Would that be okay?"

"Yes, of course. Let's go upstairs."

I took her little suitcase and I was surprised how heavy it was. "What do you have in here? It's heavy like a corpse!"

"Books! How do you know how heavy a corpse is?"

"I studied medicine." "Did you lift corpses when you studied medicine? Or carry them away?"

"No, I just saw many. I always got the impression that they were heavy. I don't know why."

"Are you a doctor?"

"No, I didn't finish my studies."

"What do you do for a living?"

"I'm a psychologist."

"Like Sigmund Freud?"

"Sort of, if you make the assumption that all psychologists are alike. But, not exactly. I'm more interested in finding out how our existence can be positively influenced by having a strong purpose in life, than knowing if someone wants to sleep with their mother or kill their father."

"That sounds ironic to me. Don't you agree with Freud?"

"He seems to reduce the human mind down to sex, and even sexuality is linked to the relationship with your parents. Is not that I don't agree with it, but I find it too simplified, for my taste."

"Sexuality?"

Was she teasing me? I opened the door of my room. "Here is my place. The toilet is over there."

She ran immediately to the toilet and I sat down on the edge of my bed, waiting for her to come out. Who was she? Was she German? Was she Jewish? Was she French? Was she an actress imitating the German accent in a cabaret, somewhere, to please the German officers who were occupying the city? Had she already identified my German accent, too? I could hear her peeing in my bathroom and I wondered why I didn't tell her to use the bathroom downstairs, as Madame Petite had told me to do. Why had I told her she could use my toilet? It seemed like she was peeing for an eternity. Then I realized I hadn't been aware before of someone else peeing. Somehow, all that this girl did I found to be interesting and I was paying attention to all the little details that were related to her. Finally, she came out.

"I feel a lot better. Could I see my room now?"

"Of course, Mademoiselle. I'll show you where it is." Her room was exactly above mine and I couldn't stop thinking about if I would hear her peeing again, maybe, from upstairs. I gave her the key and put her suitcase in her room.

"Do you like it?" "It's a little smaller than I expected. But it's okay. I don't need much."

"Do you know the neighbourhood?"

"No, I don't. Until now I have lived on the other side of Paris, quite far from here."

"Which other side? Paris is big." I tried to find out, but she didn't answer me. She looked at me as if to ask what I was still doing in her room. "Would you like me to show you the neighbourhood later? Where you might eat, for example? I know a nice bistro near here…" I plucked up the courage to ask her, although I was afraid she would reject me.

But she smiled at me again: "I would like that. Let me arrange my things first. I'm actually hungry, so I would be glad to go to that bistro."

"How much time do you need?"

"Maybe half an hour? I will knock on your door when I'm ready. Is that okay for you?"

"Oui."

I lay in bed looking at the ceiling. I was trying to hear something, but I couldn't hear anything coming from the room upstairs. I looked at the clock and when there were only two minutes left, I started to feel nervous again. The two minutes finished, but I couldn't hear her steps coming to my door. Every thirty seconds I looked at the clock. Where was she? Was she okay? Should I go and knock on her door? Maybe she was tired and had fallen asleep? After twenty minutes, when I was about to go to the kitchen to prepare myself something to eat, I heard her steps and then a firm knock.

"I thought you'd fallen asleep."

"Sorry, was I a long time? I had to clean the room, you know, to remove the dust. And then, I put my things in the wardrobe. I didn't realize it had taken so long."

"That's okay, I hadn't even noticed. I was just hungry and I was looking at the clock to see how long until we went to lunch."

"Oh, sorry, I should have said something to you. As far as I'm concerned, we can go now. I'm hungry too!"

We went to a little bistro on the corner, where I used to go whenever I wanted to eat out. I crossed my fingers the owner did not ask me how Jeanette was doing. But, well, he was French and I suppose French people know to keep their mouth shut when they see you coming with a different woman. It was a little late for lunch, so inside there was only a young couple in a corner and an old man, Monsieur Moulin, who was always sitting at the same table when I went there. The young couple had just finished their lunch, and the old man was drinking a glass of red wine and smoking a cigarette.

"Desolé, Monsieur Joseph, our kitchen is closed. You're too late."

"Don't you at least have any left-overs? We're starving! I've just met this charming young lady and I don't want to disappoint her"

"Let me ask my wife" said the owner and shouted: "Margot! Margot! Do we have something for our young Monsieur Joseph and his 'petite-amie'?"

"Cuisse de canard, je vous emprie!" shouted Margot from the kitchen.

"Ça va?" asked the owner.

"Oui, oui." I answered and I added: "And some red wine too, s'il vous plait?"

"Mais, bien-sûr."

We sat at a table in the window and the owner, Monsieur Jacques, brought us some bread and butter and two glasses of wine. Hélène started to eat with hungrily, as if she hadn't eaten for a century.

"Tell me, Mademoiselle Dubois, may I ask you what do you do for a living?"

"I give piano classes. And I study Art. The piano classes pay for university."

"Are there enough students for classes nowadays?"

"Yes, of course. People need music now more than ever. I'm maybe too busy, but it's okay. I can even save some money from time to time."

"Does the rest of your family live in Paris, too?"

"No, they don't. They live in a small village in Alsace. I have German origins. Maybe you've noticed my accent." she said whilst drinking from her glass of wine, leaving lipstick marks on it.

"Yes, I noticed. I wanted to ask you where your accent came from."

"Well, now you know. Where is your German accent from?" she asked directly. "Is my accent so obvious?"

She nodded, smiling to me kindly.

"I was also born into a German family, but in Belgium. In Wallonia."

"I thought you were born in Germany. There is something about you that reminds me of a cuisine of mine, whose family lives in the north."

At that moment, Monsieur Jacques brought us Margot's delicious 'cuisse de canard', and Hélène and I started eating immediately.

"Delicious!" remarked Hélène, satisfied. We ate silently for a while. She ate faster than me, and finished her duck leg long before I did. After cleaning her lips with a napkin, she looked around the place, especially at the paintings hanging on the walls. She seemed to be analysing each one of them in great detail.

Suddenly, she began to chuckle. At first, I thought she was laughing at me, and I was afraid that I had some food between my teeth or something, but she was actually looking at the young couple behind my back, who were kissing.

"Why are you laughing?" I asked her in a low voice, almost embarrassed; I had seen the couple before in the bistro, and they were probably regular customers, like I was.

"Every time we see French people, we assume that they are good kissers."

I glanced at the couple, trying not to stare at them, as Hélène had. "And? Don't you find they are kissing well? Do you think they are bad kissers?"

My remark seemed to make her laugh even more, because she really couldn't help herself. She was trying to answer me, but she couldn't finish her sentence because she was laughing so much. Luckily, the young couple didn't seem to notice, or they didn't care. The old man who was standing between the kissing couple and us, drank his wine undisturbed too, not paying any attention either to them, or Hélène's laughing. Finally, she stopped for a moment and said to me,

"No, no, it isn't about that couple in particular. I just think that it's absurd to think that EVERY French person is a good kisser, and other nations don't know how to do it."

"Nobody has actually said that other nations don't know how. Why do you think that?"

Monsieur Jacques interrupted us again to ask if we wanted coffee or dessert. "I only have 'coulant au chocolat' left, if you want dessert."

"Oh, that's my favourite!" said Hélène enthusiastically. "I will definitely have one!" Then she continued our conversation. "Well, nobody says that, but subconsciously we think that the French are better kissers than anybody else, don't we? The famous 'French kiss'. That implies that other nations aren't such good kissers. You should know that better than me. You're the psychologist." And she started to laugh again.

I don't know why I suddenly became frustrated. Actually I know why. I had been trying the whole afternoon to impress this girl and to get her interested in me, but there she was, looking at another couple kissing and assuming that I was a bad kisser too, simply because I wasn't French. It just infuriated me.

"Things are not so simple! You're just simplifying things." I said and I wanted to use my psychologists' tools to put her down, without even thinking that maybe she was as nervous as I was.

"Like Freud?" she chuckled. This time, her target was clearly me. That was it. Without thinking about Madame Petite, who, at that very moment, was probably crying at her sister's funeral, trusting me to behave myself with the new neighbour, I kissed Hélène. She seemed taking aback for a moment. But then, she kissed me back.

CHAPTER 21

Siegmund's diary - Schleswig-Holstein, 27th of October, 1941

After the von Hülsen family had gone, our life at the hospital went back to normal. Not that they had done anything unusual while they were there. Just that their presence itself was unusual for our modest hospital, where one would see the same old faces again and again. You couldn't really tell from inside the walls that something had changed outside those walls, or even that there was a war going on. I imagined life inside the hospital's walls twenty, thirty or forty years ago had been the same. We were like a fortress, so fortified that no enemy could get in.

Even Hermann didn't seem to bother me anymore; he was already part of the picture. I assumed he was doing his certificates for all the children, though I had never seen anything happen with those children he had examined. It looked like he was actually doing more a kind of routine, one without any consequences, and that calmed my spirit and my conscience. As long as there were no consequences, it was no use thinking of Hermann as the bad guy in the story anymore. Who knows, maybe Greta had had something to do with it, though I hadn't heard anything from her in a long while. She had never answered my note and little Hans had also vanished. But it wasn't important anymore. I had no other reason to see her otherwise. She could have vanished forever, which was okay.

Later on, Hermann also vanished. Herr Adler told me that he was very ill and couldn't come to work and wouldn't be back for an indefinite period of time. Actually, that was just perfect, because even though I didn't have any major conflicts with him, he used to assume the role of my superior and give me advice, about how should I treat my patients, patients he barely knew, without me asking for his opinion, which pissed me off. I didn't even bother to ask Herr Adler what kind of disease Hermann had; it wasn't my business, nor were we friends. It was time to go back to the peaceful life I had had before. I hadn't actually enjoyed it before, but now I was eager to have some tranquillity.

Little Werner was one of my dearest patients, despite his family's claim he was aggressive. He was rather an affectionate little fellow and everyone was happy to have him around. Herr Müller told Werner a lot of fairy tales, some of them classical, but many of them invented. The old man seemed very happy to have found someone to hear his endless stories. The boy had an insatiable appetite for them, and Herr Müller was the greatest storyteller. They seemed to be a pair made in Heaven. I even saw Herr Müller regain his good mood and energy and become the 'old Herr Müller' I had known before. I was afraid he wouldn't want to go back home anymore, at least whilst Werner was staying by us.

"What is the plan for that kid?" Herr Müller had asked me once. "How long is he going to stay with us?" Herr Müller used to say 'with us' like he was one of the regular members of staff. Given his involvement with this boy and the fact that he was like an uncle to him, he could have actually been considered one of us. We didn't do too much to Werner from a medical point of view. There was no medication to improve his condition because he was already taking Phenobarbital as part of his medication for his epileptic seizures. With us, he was neither irritable, nor aggressive, as his family had claimed. Maybe the fresh air and our hospital's tranquillity did him good.

"I don't know, Herr Müller. As far as I know, there is no plan for him. I guess he will stay here for a while, to get some rest, and one day his family will pick him up. I don't know when."

"I've heard his family has made a donation to the hospital; a big one. Herr Adler was very excited about it the other day. I think he would be able to renovate the whole hospital with it."

"I haven't heard a word about that. I had no idea! How do you know this stuff, Herr Müller? Do you listen at doors?"

"I told you, I have my sources" he winked at me with a cheeky smile. "Actually, Herr Doktor, the little chap told me."

"Werner? You mean *he* told you about the donation? And do you believe him? You know, he is only a child. And one with problems, too. Children invent things all the time. He listens to a lot of stories. You've told him many yourself, half of them invented."

"Oh, I do believe this child, Herr Doktor. I do believe him. He might have problems, as you say, but he's the cleverest boy I've ever met. Except for me, of course. He's also a cheeky little chap. If you think he has invented such things, with his fable mind, then tell me, how could a little fellow like him know about donations and similar stuff, which normally only adults talk about? Don't you think it would be more reasonable to believe that he had heard his parents talking about it, than he invented it?"

"Well, I guess you're right, Herr Müller. But he's your only source for this information, isn't he? What you say sounds reasonable, and could indeed be true, but he could have heard his parents talking about donations to other institutions or places. They are a rich family, they probably make donations all the time. I imagine Frau von Hülsen has no better way to kill her free time. So, it might be true, but we can't rule it out that it could just be something Werner made up."

"As you wish, Herr Doktor, as you wish. But I still believe the boy. And I strongly believe that they have abandoned him here. I don't think they will ever pick him up."

"I'm afraid that is my impression too, Herr Müller. And maybe you and Werner are right. Maybe his parents have made a huge donation to the hospital to be sure that we will handle Werner as if the hospital is his residence, far away from his brothers and their sophisticated life. I don't see Herr Adler anxious to see him gone. So you're probably right. I know Herr Adler is very flexible when it comes to money. It doesn't bother him that this little boy is staying here, even if there is nothing we can do for him from a medical point of view."

"People are very flexible when it comes to money: with their principles, their morals and their feelings. The more money they have, the more flexible they are willing to be. Or maybe it's that the more flexible you are, the more money you have. Who knows?"

"Well, Herr Müller, I should get back to work now. I'd love to chat with you, but I have to see my other patients too. Take care."

"Take care, Herr Doktor. I will pray to God for your heart to remain as pure and warm as it is right now. Only God knows how difficult is to keep it so, in times like these."

CHAPTER 22

Joseph's notes -Paris, 1941

After our first kiss, I felt rather detached from Hélène. It was like the full excitement I felt at the beginning had suddenly vanished after our kiss, like a spell would have been broken by the act of kissing. She became just another stranger to me, as the many strangers I had around. After all, I had just met her. I didn't know anything about her, who she really was. I suspected a lot of the things she had told me about her life were lies, and I didn't know which of her stories were true, and which were just made-up. I didn't blame her, though, for lying to me. I was lying to her myself. She probably had her reasons for not revealing her identity. That was fine. She was probably German; the more time I spent with her, the more I was convinced that my suspicions were correct. I recognized she had received the same education as I had, even if we didn't talk openly. It was like smelling a familiar perfume. You just recognize it, even if you can't put a name to it. I didn't think she was a German Jew, though, because she was too self-confident when talking to someone like me with a German accent, someone who could have easily been a threat to her. But she didn't see me as a menace, that was for sure. She was, let's say, rather condescending to me. Did she guess I was a hiding Jew? Every time we talked about my origins or my accent, she showed me excessive kindness, as if she was trying to say to me: 'Okay, I know you are Jew, but that's okay, don't worry. I'm not prejudiced. I won't turn you in. We can have a nice conversation. We can even kiss without me rejecting you or screaming that you are trying to abuse me physically or touching me without my permission'. I could see that she had a certain interest on me, because she paid attention to all the details in our conversations, which I deduced from the fact that she remembered everything afterwards. Besides, there was that kiss. I could definitely say she had kissed me back. I could even say she had kissed me back passionately, it wasn't just acceptance on her part. For a moment, I had the impression we were one. She had kissed me the way I would have kissed me myself, however odd that description sounds. Whenever I remembered us kissing, my passion for her resurfaced, exactly how I had felt it at the beginning. Sometimes, I felt even a sort of pride because I had been kissed passionately by a German woman, like it was a personal achievement. But shortly afterwards, I felt rather pathetic and ashamed of my thoughts. I remembered me reproaching my father because he hadn't fought for his position at the university. Like, he had accepted that this position had been just temporary and that he didn't actually deserve it, just because he was a Jew. And there I was, thinking that I'd achieved something because a German girl had kissed me! I was falling into the same trap, thinking that I didn't deserve to have a woman like Hélène (or whatever her real name was), because I was a Jew. It was probably a caprice for her, in a moment of curiosity about how humans around the world kiss. Our kiss should have just been the result of seeing that French couple kissing, or maybe the consequence of being in a new world, where the influences and the effects of anti-Jewish propaganda didn't sound as loud as in her home country; that new possibilities were allowed. Maybe she just wanted to experiment or add me to her long list of people she'd kissed. Or perhaps she had seen it as an opportunity to find out herself how those who lived around her kissed, since they were about to become extinct. An endangered species was what she probably thought I was. If every one of my people disappeared, that would have been quite an experience for her. I would have been a trophy; one of her achievements. And, why not? What did she have to lose? She was in a foreign country. Nobody would have judged her for what she had done with me. Nobody knew her here. Why was she there, in Paris, anyway? I guess if I had been more romantic, I would have thought she had come here because it was meant for us to meet, but I was too much of a realist at that moment of my life, too level-headed. Nothing was predestined. We were the ones who created our own destiny.

Those were exactly my thoughts on that sunny autumn afternoon, while I was resting in my bed, waiting for Hélène to get ready for a little walk along the banks of the Seine. It was a bit cold outside and Hélène just had a light jacket on. I could see she was shivering a little, but she didn't say anything. Whenever we were together, like at that moment, I felt a warm familiarity with her despite my previous thoughts. I had the impression that the Hélène I perceived when we were together and the Hélène I had in my mind when we weren't together, were slightly different. The Hélène in my mind was always self-confident and sometimes even arrogant. However, the Hélène I had by my side was open and friendly, without a hint of arrogance in her tone of voice. In my thoughts, she was sometimes ironic with me, yet in reality I could never detect any irony in her voice. I guess I was falling in love with her more and more, every time I saw her.

She took my arm and leaned her body on mine. "Do you mind if I take your arm? I'm cold.", she asked, even though I already felt her body next to mine. "Of course, Mademoiselle Hélène. Do you want my coat?"

"No, thank you. You could call me just Hélène, if you like. And I could call you just Joseph."

I smiled. I knew she was referring to our first meeting. "As you wish, Hélène." Then we walked on silently.

"Look there!" Hélène pointed at a man who was drawing on the bank of the Seine. "Isn't that the old man who drinks wine in our Bistro?"

"Mais oui, c'est Monsieur Moulin". We got closer to him and said hello.

He recognized us at once. "A, mes amis! Viens, viens!" and he showed us his drawings, which were portraits of different people of different ages. "Mademoiselle, would you like me to do your portrait?"

It was windy and I guess Hélène preferred to remain stuck to my body, but she gracefully agreed. "Mais bien-sûr, Monsieur!" and she winked at me as she sat down on a little chair.

Monsieur Moulin drew her features with a lot of dexterity; it was clear he had been doing portraits for a long time. In only five minutes Hélène's portrait was ready. He had caught her expression very well, only that in the portrait, Hélène had a touch of melancholy in her eyes. I guess it was what Monsieur Moulin had seen in her in that moment. Maybe I was the psychologist, but Monsieur Moulin had seen more faces than I had. Hélène was delighted with her portrait. After praising Monsieur Moulin's talent, she asked him how much she should pay for it.

"Mademoiselle, for you it's free. I just hope you'll keep it somewhere, and pass it on to your children one day, a little memory from an old man. If I were still young, like Monsieur Joseph, I would court you, for sure. At least, this is something an old man could give you. So take it." Hélène took it, thanked Monsieur Moulin and then kissed him on his cheek. Monsieur Moulin smiled and we continued our walk in silence.

It crossed my mind that we could walk like this for a lifetime. Then I remembered that I was a Jew and she was a German and I started to imagine scenarios where we talked openly to each other. In case I was wrong, and she didn't actually suspect anything, what would her reaction be? The thought that she might laugh at me, suddenly disregard me, or even hate me because I had dared to kiss her, made me freeze: I couldn't feel my feet and I felt a lump in my throat. Then I started to wonder why I was making such a fuss over that girl. She was beautiful and well educated and it seemed that there was a connection between us, although, there were many other girls, French girls, who were at least as interesting as Hélène. If they didn't have exactly her qualities, they had many others to compensate. The feeling that I was with the love of my life, someone really unique, I had had again and again at the beginning of every relationship with every girl that I'd fallen in love with. It was just the way it was. I was probably influenced by the excitement of a new experience more than by genuine feelings for someone. I was sure that, in a few months' time, I would find another Hélène somewhere, without complicating my life too much. And if she turned me in, if she found out? What would her family have said about us? Could I accept her family too? I should have probably be the one to reject her and her family, given what her people had done to my father, who I knew nothing of anymore. Was he still alive? My attempts to find out if my family was still alive had come to nothing, and I didn't want to go back to Germany. It made no sense. The only thing which would happen is that I would be caught and sent to a concentration camp. Not even France was a safe place anymore. Immigrating to the United States would have been safer. The only reasonable thing to do was to cut myself off from my old life, including Paris and the questionable relationship with Hélène, and to run away again, as far away as possible from my past. With Hélène, it was probably just physical attraction. Yes, that is exactly what it was, which would have explained why I always felt something for her only when she was around, and that I was completely detached when I was alone. There was no reason to stay in Paris anymore.

However, I did nothing. Each day it crossed my mind that I should pack and flee, but the time passed and I was still there. After two weeks or so, a friend of mine said to me that he and his sister were going to Nice to enjoy the good weather before the winter came, and they invited me to go with them. I thought it would be a good idea to invite Hélène too, as company for Mireille, my friend's sister. After all, Hélène didn't seem to have any social life, except for going out with me from time to time. A little fresh sea air would do her good. I had the impression she had lost weight and she was a bit pale; probably giving piano classes all around Paris and going to the university at the same time was exhausting for her.

"Joseph, oh, that would be nice, but I can't. I have too many things to do, believe me. I can't allow myself to lose any students. I'm sorry, maybe next time. Thank you anyway for your invitation. It's nice of you that you thought of me."

"Do you think you will lose your students if you disappear for a couple of weeks? Come on, I'm sure your students are so happy with you, that they wouldn't give up on you just for that. It will be fun. And you need some rest. You're pale, you work too much."

"No, Joseph, I can't. Next time."

I still tried to insist, but she was categorical. There was no sense in insisting. She went to her room, pretending that she was exhausted and needed some sleep.

After an half an hour, I heard a shy knock on my door. "May I come in?" she asked.

"Yes, of course, Hélène, come in." She came in, but remained at the door. It was clear she wanted to say something to me, but she couldn't find the words. Then she started to cry.

"Hélène? What's wrong? Come, sit down. Do you want a glass of water?"

She shook her head. "I don't want you to be upset with me because I can't come to Nice with you."

"Upset? That's a silly thought, Hélène. Why should I be upset?"

"You don't know me. I'm not who I say I am." and she paused. "I can't lie to you anymore, Joseph. I don't want to lie to you. But it's difficult for me to tell you who I am. You won't want to talk to me anymore. Probably..." I took a deep breath. So the moment of true had come. It made sense. Either we talked openly, or we said goodbye to each other. Maybe it had also been a reason for me deciding what to do next with my life. Why did I think of her when it came to deciding what to do next with my life anyway? Well, I guess, sometimes we don't question our destiny too much and just accept it.

She went on: "My name isn't Hélène Dubois, but Greta Adler. Actually Greta Wagner. I'm a German, married to an SS general. I ran away from home, from my husband. I never wanted to marry him anyway, but I was, let's say, forced to do it. I didn't have any other choice. My only choice was to run away. I waited for the best moment to do it. I had to cut myself off from my whole life in Germany and my family."

She looked at me to see my reaction. I was perplexed, not because I wouldn't have guessed that she was German, but it had never crossed my mind that Greta was married and she had run away from home.

"Go on, I'm listening."

"Are you still my friend, Joseph? You're the only friend I have here."

"Hélène, I mean Greta. I've always had the suspicion that you were German. I mean, not just a French girl with German origins. But, you must understand that I'm surprised."

"I know, but I thought it would be better to put my cards on the table. I wanted to study art. If it hadn't been for the war, my father would have probably sent me to study here in Paris anyway. Joseph, I also have suspicions about you. I think you're a Jew. Your name isn't exactly the best cover for you."

"It's my real name."

"I thought so." and she smiled. "Did you escape from Germany?"

"A long time ago. It's a long story."

"Do you have family here? You don't have to answer me. I would understand if you didn't trust me. I mean, I'm German and I've already lied to you."

"I don't have any family here. I don't know where they are now. I try not to think about it."

We looked at each other for a while, without saying anything. I suddenly felt good inside. As if I was at peace. I didn't know at that moment why, but I guess it had something to do with my decision to remain in Paris.

"I think I should go upstairs now. I guess you need time to think about what I've just told you and assimilate it." She was about to leave when she turned around to me and said: "I guess, I would be sad if you didn't want to speak to me anymore. Which is what will probably happen. I guess I'm not a lucky girl."

"Greta, would you like to go to Nice with me? I would be happy if you accepted."

"I told you that I can't, Joseph. If there's a next time, I will be happy to." "Maybe you could stay fewer days, than the rest of us? Just three or four."

"I can't. Good night." and she went upstairs.

I laid on my bed, looking at the ceiling and thinking about all the information she had told me. Was she telling the truth now? There was no reason to invent all that. The fact she was married, and to an SS general, too, had definitely taken me aback. But I was so happy that we had finally spoken openly to each other. If she had been my enemy, she would have already turned me in, and she wouldn't have confessed her past to me. And slowly I began to realize: she was me. I mean, she was like me. She wanted so badly to study the arts that she had given up her comfortable life as an SS general's wife, to live in modest conditions, giving piano classes to earn a living. She hadn't even been forced to do it, she had *chosen* to do it. Greta had a strong purpose in life and that was reflected in her life: coming to Paris, studying art, getting to know me…

I ran upstairs and I knocked at her door.

"Greta, I want to talk to you."

"About what? It's late. It'd better if we talked tomorrow."

"I want to ask you something, Greta."

"What? I'm not going to come to Nice with you, if that is what you want to ask."

"I want to ask you to marry me."

"To marry you? I can't marry you, silly! I'm already married. I wasn't lying to you about that. I'm German and I'm married to an SS general, exactly as I told you."

"That is exactly why I want to marry you!"

"Because I'm an SS general's wife? This is why you want to marry me?"

"No, I mean you gave up everything, to follow your goal. Your life was comfortable, wasn't it? I guess you didn't live in a small room like this, did you?"

"It doesn't matter anymore, Joseph. What it was like before is already gone for me. I have a new life and this is my new life."

"I want to be a part of your life, Greta. I don't have anything behind me, either. I don't care you are German. And I'm sure a good lawyer could get a divorce for you."

At that moment, I had the feeling that someone was standing behind me. I turned around and I saw Madame Petite. She had probably been standing there for a while, but I had been so excited that I hadn't noticed her. She was trembling.

"I want no Germans in my house! She must go right now! Out, out of my house right now!" and Madame Petite went to open Greta's door with a key.

"But Madame Petite, you don't understand! She ran away from home to come here! To study art! To study art in Paris! She gave up everything. She told me the truth. She didn't turn me in either!"

"I don't care why she came to Paris, she can't stay in my house!"

"But why? She is on our side. She hasn't hurt anyone."

"*Our* side? Do you think you are on my side? Just because you've found a home here, and you were well treated by all of us, and nobody sends you to a concentration camp? Do you think that makes you one of us? Are you French? Have you ever suffered together with us? Was your family here when we struggled with *our* problems? Did you lose a child to this damn war? Do you know how it feels? These bloody Germans! They stole our land once, Alsace-Lorraine, those thieves, and now they want to steal it from us again. I won't help any of them! Out of my house, or I'll call the police and turn you both in. I'm sure her husband would be happy to have her back. Go back to Germany, where you come from, bloody liar!"

Greta came out. "It's useless, Joseph. Give me ten minutes, Madame Petite, to pack my stuff. I'll go."

"I come with you, Greta, wherever you go. I just want to be with you."

"You can go too, Monsieur Joseph! You and your German whore!"

When we went downstairs it was almost night and raining. I didn't know where to go. A motel? They would have asked us less questions than in a decent hotel. They might think that we were there just for sex. The next day we would have to figure it out. Nice wasn't probably a bad idea, after all.

"Where are you going, my friends?" asked Monsieur Moulin.

"Je sais pas, Monsieur Moulin. Je sais pas..."

"Venez! Venez avec moi!" and seeing that we hadn't moved, he insisted. "Mais venez mes amis!" As if we were hypnotized, we followed him. He took us to a small apartment he had just around the corner. He poured us some cognac.

"You can stay here. My place is small, but I have a little room for you two. I guess you don't need more than that."

"Why are you helping us, Monsieur Moulin?"

"Well, because once I wanted to study art in Paris, like this little lady here wants to. It was after Germany had taken Alsace and Lorraine from France. I didn't know I wouldn't be welcome here." and he winked. "But now I know. I could never study art. We don't want the same to happen to this pretty lady."

"Are you German, Monsieur Moulin?"

"Oui, oui…You wouldn't guess it, would you? After so many years, I've even lost my accent. Can you believe that my surname was actually Müller? When I came to France, I changed it to Moulin." and he winked again. "German, French…who knows anymore? Born and raised in Germany. Fifty years I've spent in Paris, since I was still a young man. I don't know what I am, anymore. I guess only God can say for sure now."

CHAPTER 23

Joseph's notes -Paris, 1941

The next morning someone nocked loudly on Monsieur Moulin's door. Then we heard men voices speaking in German. Greta and I looked at each other. Neither of us said a word. I just held her tight in my arms, as if I wanted her to get inside me, for protection.

"But they're my son and his wife, putain!" we heard Monsieur Moulin saying in German. "They live in Nice, and have come to visit me for a week. What evidences do you want from us? I can show you their passports, to prove their identities. Let me see if they're awake yet."

And then we heard a knock on our bedroom door. "Germain! Germain! Some officers from the Gestapo are here. They want to see you and Hélène and your passports. Are you both awake?"

We didn't make a sound, because we didn't know what to say. We definitely didn't have any passports showing that I was Monsieur Moulin's son, and Greta was my wife. Why had he told such a lie? There was no way to prove that the three of us were related.

"Open the door, Germain, or I have to come inside myself! I'm sure these officers have others things to do, you know. They can't wait for you and Hélène to groom yourselves and have breakfast!" And he opened the door. "Just a moment!" he said to the officers.

Monsieur Moulin stepped in, and he put a finger to his lips so that we remained quiet. Then he opened a cupboard and took out two passports. Before he went out, he told us to put some cloths on and come outside: "Those officers want to see you in person, I'm afraid".

After Monsieur Moulin had left the room, Greta whispered: "What if my husband has given my photo to the Gestapo? What if they recognize me, Joseph?"

"I'm afraid we have to go and talk to them anyway, Greta. If not, they will surely come inside, and if they already suspect something, it'll be worse. We have no other choice. We have to take the risk and go outside."

"But I'm sure they will recognize me. I'm sure Hermann is already looking for me, and I'm sure has given all of his photos of me to the Gestapo. I tried to take some of them with me, but I know he carries one of me in his pocket; one of me before we got married, which my father gave him."

"If we don't go to talk to them soon, they will get very suspicious, Greta. Let's take one more risk. We've already taken some before, haven't we?"

Greta got dressed and tried to arrange her hair differently, in a bun, holding the bun together with a pencil she had found on the desk. Then she looked into my eyes again.

"Joseph, if they discover that you are a Jew, and they want to send you to a concentration camp, and that I'm Greta Wagner, and send me back to my husband in Germany, would you die with me?"

"Like Romeo and Juliet?"

"Yes."

I wanted to tell her that I didn't want to die right then, now that I had found her, and my life had meaning again. But I knew that she was waiting for different answer from me, and we didn't have time for any further discussions.

"Yes", I answered.

Then someone knocked loudly at the door. "May we come in?" someone asked in German, and before we had time to say anything, the door just opened.

There were three officers, one of whom looked like their superior. He had the two passports Monsieur Moulin had given them, and he stared at us for a while.

"Your names, please?" he asked.

As if I was in a trance again, exactly like the night before, when Monsieur Moulin had brought us to his home, I answered: "Germain Moulin, Herr officer. And this is my wife, Hélène."

"And do you expect me to believe that?" he asked.

"I've told you our names, as you asked me for. Why do you ask me for my name, if you don't want to believe it anyway?"

"Germain, don't upset him." whispered Greta.

"Why do you suspect that we aren't who we say we are?" I continued.

"Monsieur Moulin -or wherever your name is- I'm in charge of asking questions here, not you!"

"As a French citizen I have the right to ask whatever I want, of course, and to defend myself, when my identity is called into question! The fact that you invaded our country, doesn't mean that you can treat us the way you do, without any respect! We still have our rights! I'm sure your own superiors told you that you should treat us, French citizens, right. Do you want me to complain about you, to your superiors, Officer? That you have come into my bedroom, uninvited, and insulted me and my wife, who was half naked?" I continued in an offended tone, on the presumption that the passports that Monsieur Moulin had given them, which apparently showed our false names in them, depicted two French citizens.

"Shut up, Monsieur!" cried the officer. "We were told that last night Monsieur Moulin had brought two strangers to his home in the middle of the night. It's our duty to search for fugitive Jews. If you interfere with our procedures, I can throw you in jail, if I want to!"

"Mais c'est inacceptable!" I burst out.

"Germain, calme-toi!" said Hélène. "You must excuse my husband for his behaviour, Herr officer, but he has lost a lot of money on gambling in the last months, and he has had a break-down. He has also become addicted to alcohol because he lost all our savings. That's why we came here. We hoped that my father-in-law would loan us some money to buy a little vineyard and start a new business. We're broke and my husband has become a drunk."

"You, French people! Always losing money on gambling, wine and women! And do you really think it's a good idea to buy a vineyard, after all?"

"Yes, Herr Officer." said Hélène charmingly. My father had a little vineyard in Alsace-Lorraine, but he died very young because of the Spanish flu. My mother sold it, because she didn't know what to do with it. I loved that little vineyard and when I was a little girl I spent a lot of time with my father and his grapes. I learnt a lot about wines from my father, and I'm sure starting a new business with my husband could save our marriage too. For us, French people, wine means love. This is what makes our wines so special."

The officer looked at us again and then burst out laughing. "Come on, guys, let's go!" he said to the other two. "When the war is over, I will move here and buy myself a little vineyard, too. 'Wine means love', who would have thought that? Only French people are capable of making poetry out of booze."

After the three officers went out I looked at Monsieur Moulin astonished. "Monsieur Moulin, how did you do that? How did you have the two passports already prepared with false names in them? Are you a magician?"

"An old man is always prepared for everything. You'll see when you get old. At my age God tells you things which your ears were not prepared to listen before." and he winked at me like a wise child who didn't want to betray the secret his best friend had asked him not to. "When I was your age, I just believed in rationality and facts, too. I thought I was the only one in charge of my own life, but I never actually have been, at least not completely. We can only choose the moves we make, not their final result. And sometimes you don't make any move at all, but still get the best thing you could have only imagined before. Look at your pretty lady here." and he winked again, looking at Greta. Greta smiled and winked back, as if they shared a story I wasn't aware of. And for a moment, probably because of the way he winked at me, I had the odd impression that I had known Monsieur Moulin from another life, or maybe from a different story. A story where I was still in Germany, working as a doctor in a country hospital near Kiel (the place where I had seen Siegmund for the last time, before I took off for France) and Monsieur Moulin (or Herr Müller, by his real name) was an old friend who came to visit me from time to time and cheer me up with his funny stories. Despite the foolishness of my thought, giving the impossibility of being a free Jew working in Germany at that time, weirdly, it felt like that to me. But this strange thought vanished immediately and I just wondered how my life would have been if I hadn't had the urge to flee Germany before the war started. Should I consider myself blessed? How could I cope with the guilty feeling that I've never said goodbye to my parents, at least? Herr Müller looked at me as if he had read my thoughts. He sighed. "Well, you may officially consider yourself my son now, if you like. I've never had one, so you'd make an old man very happy. You and your lovely wife are my family now. At least this is what your passports say." And then he added carefully: "I know I'll never replace your family. Please don't take my proposal as a lack of consideration for your feelings for them. Take it as a dear wish of an old man." Greta took my hand and caressed my fingers. "Herr Müller, none of us has a family anymore. My folks are probably still alive, but I lost any contact with them. You've made us your family. You can do magic, indeed." said Greta thoughtfully. "I wish I could do more magic, but my powers are limited, I'm afraid." he added, and I found certain sadness in his voice.

CHAPTER 24

Siegmund's diary - Schleswig-Holstein, 24th of December 1941

On 24th of December 1941, while we were changing over shifts, the nurse who had been on the night shift told us that the previous night Werner had been extremely agitated. When the staff had tried to check on him, he had become aggressive towards them and bit her. They hadn't been able to do much to calm him down, and so they had tied him to the bed with some rope.

"Hmmm", mumbled Herr Adler. "Has this ever happened before?"

"As far as I know, no." answered the nurse.

"So he is aggressive, after all, and a threat to others, exactly as his parents told us he was." added Herr Adler and he involuntarily touched his beard, as he did when he was thinking about a decision he was going to take.

"Was he agitated in his sleep? Could it be that he was only enacting his dreams?" I asked.

"I can't tell." answered the nurse.

"Why can't you tell? Was he awake, or not?"

"What difference does that makes?" intervened Herr Adler. "That boy is aggressive. He bites people! We can't allow something like this to happen. His parents have already warned us about him."

"Herr Adler," I started, trying to keep my voice down, "maybe the boy has 'night terrors'. Maybe he's not aggressive and he's just acting out his dreams whilst asleep. I've seen this boy every day since he has been here, and I've never seen him be aggressive. He's actually a quiet loving boy. All the other patients here are happy to have him around."

"Well, but he was aggressive last night, wasn't he? He bit the nurse! What more do you want? Could you show us, Fräulein, where this boy bit you?" asked Herr Adler intrigued.

The nurse came closer and showed us a little mark she had on her finger.

"That's repulsive!" said Herr Adler. "How can a human being bite another? Shall we still call them human beings?" said Herr Adler disgusted.

"But Herr Adler, children bite each other when they are playing sometimes or even hit each other too. And perhaps Werner was asleep. Who knows what he was dreaming? Night terrors are relative frequent in children and they don't have anything to do with his cerebral palsy."

"Who said his aggression has anything to do with his cerebral palsy? You are mixing things up, Herr Berg!"

"But I don't think the boy is aggressive at all, Herr Adler- this is exactly what I'm trying to say. One can't say he's aggressive just because he's agitated while sleeping, even if he did bite the nurse. I'm sure he wasn't even aware of it."

"Are they ever aware of their aggressiveness? Aren't they all alike? I worked in a psychiatric clinic in Berlin, and I know for sure that they are never aware of what they do when they are psychotic. It's a symptom of the disease itself."

"But this child, I know him! I've seen him every day and he's not psychotic."

"Herr Berg, that's enough! You weren't here last night, were you? So you don't actually know what happened. However, you think that only your opinion counts. There were others here who saw him. Why should I believe you, and not them?"

"Because I'm the doctor, Werner's doctor! I don't think anyone who was here last night has ever heard of night terrors, or know how to recognize them. Not even his parents."

"Enough, Herr Berg! Now you offend us all! You act as you are the expert here. A little modesty doesn't harm anyone. Now the discussion is over. I'll see what we can do about this boy."

I went to see Werner right away and Herr Müller was there too, talking to him. The boy was calmly listening to Herr Müller and smiled at me when I came in.

"How is my favourite little patient, today?" I asked. "Did you sleep well, little fellow?"

"Aha." he answered and laughed.

"Did you have a bad dream last night? Can you remember it?"

"Aha." repeated Werner.

"What was the dream about, little friend?"

"Aha." repeated Werner and laughed again.

"Werner, it's important to tell me anything about your dream last night, even a word or two. I'm sure you remember something."

"Horse" said Werner.

"Did you dream about a horse?"

"Aha."

"Was he a nice horse, or a bad horse?"

"Aha, horse"

"Were you afraid of the horse, Werner? Was he a bad horse?"

"Aha, big horse, black horse."

"Do you remember anything else, Werner? Do you know that you screamed and a nurse was here?"

"Aha."

"Do you remember biting the nurse?"

"Aha."

"Why did you do that? Was she mean to you? Did she yell at you?"

Werner laughed. It was useless. It was impossible to find out from him what happened.

"I was here." said Herr Müller.

"I think the boy was asleep. I know because he wasn't himself anymore. When I said his name aloud, several times, he seemed to wake up, and then he was like he is right now."

"This is what I think too, Herr Müller. Only, nobody believes us…"

After that, I went to see other patients. When I came back to my office the secretary came and told me that Herr Adler wanted to talk to me.

"Don't you ever contradict me in front of others again, Herr Berg. I have already had enough from you. I have tried to protect you, not to turn you in to the authorities. I've done everything in my power to promote you in my clinic, but that's enough."

"Herr Adler, I only tried to give the correct diagnostic of Werner. I haven't ever seen him be aggressive, and as I haven't seen it with my own eyes, I can't be sure that what he had wasn't acting out his dream. I think he deserves a fair chance; he's only a child."

"A fair chance? What are you talking about? What are we, judges? Is this a court here? I wasn't aware that we were judging Werner. Listen to me, Herr Berg. What that boy needs is an appropriate treatment. His medication is clearly not working. I don't know what you have done up to now; whatever it is, it hasn't worked. If Herr Wagner were ill, he would have taken good care of boy, but unfortunately he's not here, and you have to handle him. Listen to me carefully. I'm not interested in your opinion anymore. I just want you to listen and to do exactly what I tell you to do with this boy. Herr Wagner wrote that the boy becomes aggressive whenever he's in pain. Morphine should relieve his pain, and with it, his irritability. It's a pity that you couldn't figure out yourself that this boy is in pain. He's retarded, so he can't say it aloud himself. But you, as his doctor, should have known better."

"Hermann only saw Werner once. Werner is not in pain. I know that better than Hermann, after seeing him every day."

"There we go again, Herr Berg? Does only *your* opinion count here? Hermann has dealt with a lot more children than you, and has more experience than you have with this disease, for Christ's sake! I don't doubt Herr Wagner's evaluation for a moment. Not to mention that he's your superior. Did you read the boy's file? Did you read what Herr Wagner wrote in it?"

"The fact that Herr Wagner is a general doesn't make him my superior. His medical knowledge has nothing to do with his military rank. I read what Herr Wagner wrote, but as his peer, I can question his opinion. I wouldn't give Werner as higher dose as Hermann recommended in his file. He is not in pain, and even if he was, the dose recommended by Hermann would kill him. We both know that, Herr Adler, don't we? This is why the boy was brought here from the beginning, isn't it? All the rest are just inventions."

"How dare you! How dare you, Herr Berg, put my ethics into question? How could you still think that your judgement counts more than mine, or Herr Wagner's, whose opinion corresponds with mine? Don't you see that *you* are the only one whose convictions aren't compatible with ours? Don't you ever take into consideration that you're actually the one who's wrong? I'll accept your resignation right now. I understand that your incompatibility with the rest of us means you don't want to work here with us anymore. Good bye, Herr Berg. I hope you'll find your way in life."

I was just about to leave Herr Adler's office, when suddenly the image of my son, Arthur, came into my mind. What if someday he was be in the same situation as Werner? Would anyone bother to fight for his life, or would he just be abandoned to his cruel fate? I was the only one in the hospital who had stood up for Werner. Nobody else seemed to care about him except Herr Müller, who had even less power than I had. If I hadn't taken a stand at that moment, what would have happened to Werner? So, instead of going, I turned around to Herr Adler and said:

"If anything happens to Werner, I am going to report you for helping Jews by inventing medical reasons to enable them to escape to Denmark."

"What are you saying, Herr Berg? Have you lost your mind? Why are you saying such nonsense?"

"You know very well why, Herr Adler. I was involved in helping two of them. You sent us to Denmark and I was complicit. I don't care what happens to me, but I do care when it comes to what happens to Werner."

Herr Adler started to laugh out loud. "You've clearly lost your mind, Herr Berg! You're just angry that you have to leave the hospital, and threatening me with your made-up stories. Please do yourself a favour and don't make your situation any worse. You have no idea what you're doing to yourself right now."

"They are not made-up stories, and we both know it. The Eichels were Jews, and you sent them to Denmark. I still have the letter you gave me to show to the officers at the border. It's signed by you."

"And? What does that letter prove? The Eichels weren't Jews! It just said that you were escorting a patient and his father to Denmark. What else does it prove?"

"But they were Jews! I know it! I'm sure anyone who looks in the archives for their names will find their origins."

"Herr Berg, you are now acting irresponsibly and childishly. You're threatening me with a nonsense story you can't actually prove. Think about your son. Have you thought what his life would be like if they find out you're homosexual? Think about it for a minute."

"What do you mean, Herr Adler? I'm not homosexual. You have no proof either."

Herr Adler laughed again. "Of course, I have no proof! But I don't need any proof to expose you. Many of my employees think the same as I do, and they will be glad to back me up, if I ask them to. We don't need any evidence to prove that you're homosexual if the majority claim it. It's as simple as that. I'm afraid you've gone too far, Herr Berg."

And then Herr Adler paused, looking deep into my eyes. It was the first time in many months that I had the impression that he had that paternal attitude toward me again. "Look, Herr Berg. Personally, I don't have anything against you. I don't particularly like you guys, but someone's private life is their business, not mine. I've always thought that way. Ten years ago, nobody would have held it against you, or your personal choices. We've been always open-minded people when it comes to sexual orientation, far more than the rest. But now the regime has changed. You were born too late, Herr Berg. Homosexuality is considered a crime under the new regime, and there is nothing you or I can do about it. Everyone has to survive somehow and have to adapt to the new regime. Haven't you already realised that it's useless to fight? Tell me, who are you fighting against, Herr Berg? A whole nation?"

I felt a cold sweat and clenched my hands. I knew he was right. Herr Adler was a pragmatic man, and I'd always known that.

"Go home, Herr Berg. Go home to your son. I hope God will take care of your soul. There is nothing more I can do to help you."

Two days after, I met Herr Müller. He told me that Werner had been found dead the previous day. He had died in his sleep. He had probably been dead for several hours when the staff came to wake him up in the morning. The rumours Herr Müller had heard, were that the nurse had given Werner the dose of morphine I had told her to give him, the last time I had examined Werner.

EPILOGUE

Christa's notes - Barcelona, 2008

Joseph and I agreed to meet in Plaza Cataluña at 7 pm. It was too soon to have dinner, but actually the aim of our meeting was to do the last interview for my book. I was about to finish it and there were just a couple more things that I wanted to know from him, before sending my novel to the editor. I felt nervous. He was the last character of my book to whom I must say good-bye. The moment had come.

"Good afternoon, Christa. Nice to see you again."

"Nice to see you again too, Joseph. How are you? Did you have a good flight?"

"Yes, actually I slept the whole flight. I woke up as we landed. Since the last time, I've been feeling a bit tired. I sleep better at night, which is good. And you? Have you done anything interesting since we last met?"

"Not really. I've done a lot of things, but I don't think any of them are notable. Just routine."

"You'll probably laugh, but most of my life I've felt the same as you, that my life is just routine. However, most of the people I've met have found my life story to be exciting."

"You're probably right, Joseph. We sometimes miss seeing how unique our lives are; or at least, interesting. Everyone has a different story to tell. Well, I've prepared a long list of questions for our interview. One of them is for my book, the others just for my curiosity. I hope this time you'll answer all my questions."

"I'll try. I think the moment to answer your questions has now come."

"So, Joseph, I am going to start with my first question: how did you find me after our first interview? How did you know that I was living in Barcelona and where did you get my private email address from?"

"I gave your first name and surname to my grandson, who works for an email service company in California, and he located you and gave me the other information about you I'd asked him for."

"How is that possible? Shouldn't our personal data be confidential?"

"The email service companies have access to the entire personal data of their clients, including the contents of their private mails."

"To be sure that everyone understands. What you've just said is that, for example, they could read the emails I have sent to you, and the ones you have sent to me?"

"Exactly."

"You asked me not to give your real surname in my book, in order to protect your grandson's identity. May I use the name 'Miller' for your surname in my novel?"

"Of course. You can use Miller, Müller or Moulin, as you like. I guess all of them suit me."

"So, Mr. Miller, why did you contact me and ask me to write this book?"

"Because people are not aware that their private sphere has been broken, and for ethical reasons I think everyone should be aware of. I've felt on my own skin what the consequences of propaganda can be and I'm afraid the proportion of people's mind manipulated through social media is on a much bigger scale nowadays than it has ever been before."

"What does the fact that these email service company have access to our personal information have to do with propaganda and manipulation?"

"Imagine someone has access to your personal thoughts and opinions, so that they can deduce what your tastes are, the frequency you write to a certain person, the hours you are awake and using the internet, where you work, what you do, the web pages you access most frequently on the internet and your browsing habits. Imagine someone having all that information, basically knowing everything about you. They would then be in a position to offer you things you're unlikely to refuse based on your online psychological profile. It'd be like an internet Trojan horse. Wouldn't it be the perfect way to manipulate you?"

"You said that is not the commercial part that worries you, but the political consequences. What exactly do you mean by that?"

"Well, it means that people might be determined to vote for a person based on propaganda via social media. What I, personally, find sad, is the fact that the reason for voting or not for a certain politician may have more to do with frivolities than with their political platform. For example, let's say that the physical appearance of a certain politician resembles Donald Duck. Imagine that someone, on the internet who wants to convince you to vote in a certain way, or just in order to make a joke, constantly associates the picture of that politician with that of Donald Duck. You've seen the two pictures together over and over, with a new comment underneath every day, both also having similar personalities. Apparently inoffensive stuff. Your friends also express their opinions about the association between these two 'Donalds', and in time an opinion, for or against, will be formed. You will be asked about your opinion, but actually it will be more like a suggestion that your opinion should correspond to the general opinion that has emerged on the internet. Since we are social animals and our desire to feel integrated in society is one of our primordial needs, there is a strong probability you'll embrace that opinion, even if it doesn't totally match your viewpoint. In the end, people will vote for that politician based on their sympathy or antipathy to Donald Duck. Furthermore, even wars can be started because of it. Now it's easier than ever to start conflicts between different groups."

"Because of Donald Duck?"

"Because of similar trivial reasons, it could be Donald Duck, Goofy, or who knows, tomorrow it could be Mickey Mouse. Who would vote for a candidate who is constantly associated with Goofy on social media? First of all, your civic responsibility wouldn't allow it, and then, even if you wanted to vote for Goofy, your other 'friends' on the internet would say 'How can you vote for Goofy if you're one of us?'. That's why I find social media one of the most anti-democratic vehicles for sharing and spreading information nowadays. Groups are already prone to hate each other and have conflicts, every group looking for supremacy. We are already born with a 'herd instinct'. Acting from instinct means acting without reasoning; it's an impulse, an urge to do things. Trivial triggers like Donald or Goofy, related constantly to things that are really important to us, can bring our 'fight or flight' instinct to the surface. This is what propaganda is based on. We forget that democracy means making free choices."

"Nevertheless, propaganda has been used throughout the history of humanity and people have always found one way or another to positively or negatively influence other people's opinions. There are well-known books that have changed history. Giving only a few examples: the Bible, "Thus spoke Zarathustra", Machiavelli's "The Prince", "Uncle's Tom Cabin", Marx's "The Capital". Why do you think there is a bigger danger nowadays of people being manipulated than there was before?"

"A book gives you at least the possibility to reason. Reading, at least, appeals to one of the superior functions in the brain. I would say that every time a book has led to conflicts between people, it was because of the misinterpretation of its content. It wasn't the content itself, but the fact that someone spread false ideas to those who haven't actually read the book, but just heard an interpretation; as always, people's ignorance of a certain subject."

"Don't you think what you are saying sounds radical? Aren't you assuming that people generally don't reason when taking a decision, and are only influenced by their instincts? Isn't that a generalization, after all?"

"I admit what I'm saying might sound radical. I am also aware that what I say might upset people. But this is the only possible way to have an impact on what others think. The louder things are said, the more impact they have. Things said in a low voice don't reach anyone's ears. This is what propaganda is based on. It's not necessary to say only nice things. You can say ugly things too, but loud enough. Then, people will listen to."

"Do you think there is anything we can do to avoid falling into this trap - the trap of believing everything that is said, showed or promoted on the internet? Is there any way one can avoid being influenced by propaganda?"

"Propaganda appeals mostly to our feelings, not our reasoning. Fear and anger are the most frequent targets. Whenever news or speeches make you afraid or angry, take a breath and try to think about if what is said is true or not. It could be true, no doubt, but you won't know as long as you're being influenced by your emotions. You know you are reasoning when you feel emotionally detached."

"You said before that books appeal to our reasoning, and that's why they are not as dangerous as the frivolous propaganda on the internet is. What do you have to say about Adolf Hitler's 'Mein Kampf'? Do you think we can consider it inoffensive, just because it's a book?"

Joseph laughs.

"You've got me on that one. Well, I think this book could be included in the category of judgments based on anger and fear. And hate too. It has more to do with sentimentalism and frustration than reasoning."

"You say that reasoning and a lack of emotions are the key to avoiding conflicts between groups. Isn't a lack of emotions a sign of mental illness? We are human beings. How could we be detached from our feelings? Isn't it just a way of fooling ourselves? Don't you think the lack of emotional involvement leads to even worse atrocities? What about love, empathy, joy, hope or solidarity? Should we ignore them as well?"

"Emotions are definitely part of our *'psyche'*, nobody can doubt that. But, (and this is my personal opinion after all) our 'duty' as reasoning beings is to learn to recognize them, at least, and to be aware about which of our decisions have been made based on emotions."

"Don't you think this book is a type of propaganda too, after all? Propaganda against social media? Or propaganda against propaganda?"

"The term 'propaganda' comes from 'propagare', meaning 'to spread'. I guess, we can't formally talk about propaganda when something hasn't been propagated. I would let your readers decide if this is propaganda or not. However, what I personally want to transmit is that people shouldn't hate each other for reasons that aren't theirs. Of course, this raises a moral dilemma: is it right or wrong to use propaganda for good? My personal opinion is that it's not moral, because nobody is in possession of the absolute truth. I guess, in the majority of cases, when someone wants to influence others, they think they are doing it for the right reasons. And history has demonstrated that it wasn't. What I would like, actually, is to give others something to think about, for them to see things from my perspective, whilst still keeping their own."

"Do you find yourself represented in this book, Joseph?"

"I think many people can find themselves represented in this book. These things aren't only happening on a large scale, or just in a certain historical context. Discrimination isn't just about killing people in concentration camps, humiliating them on the streets, or not allowing them to have dinner in certain restaurants. Things are sometimes a lot more subtle than that. Sometimes it's only about not giving a fair chance to everyone to fulfil their own destiny. I was told that I should consider myself lucky because I wasn't directly affected by the Holocaust, since I'd escaped from Germany before the deportation began. There were people who have even argued about how much influence Nazi propaganda had on my own destiny, because I didn't suffer any physical harm and somehow I still managed to succeed in life. Should I consider myself lucky? In documentaries, we only see the damage caused by malnutrition, exhaustion, separation from your family, or genocide. People are only sensitive to stories about not fulfilling basic needs. But we are a lot more than our basic needs. We want to accomplish something in our life and leave a trace after our deaths. We are the only animals conscious of our own death and want to leave something behind. We are the only ones trying to give our lives meaning, the only ones dreaming about eternity and capable of imagining a life after death. We are trying desperately to maintain our memory alive, even after our mundane existence is over. Not allowing someone to fulfil their potential is a way of killing them, from a philosophical point of view. I don't mean physically, of course. If you want to destroy someone, just take something from them they have accomplished in their life, and they will probably want to die. Like the old Eichel, who committed suicide, though he still had the chance to escape from Denmark to England before Denmark was invaded by the Germans. But he didn't find any meaning in his existence anymore, and, therefore, no reason to live. There are other examples, like the painters Anita Reé and Ernst Ludwig Kirchner, who committed suicide for the same reason, but who the media doesn't talk about. Moreover, the real reason they committed suicide wasn't depression, as is commonly reported, but because they had been unable to fulfil their reason for being, in Eichel's case his son and for the artists, the pursuit of their art.

"Well, maybe I've failed to highlight this in my novel. I don't seem to have included this theme in my book, as you would like to."

"I don't think it's necessary to insist on that. People would get bored quickly if you insisted on only one topic.

"I've noticed that the names of your characters have certain meanings in the context of the story. For example, 'Eichel' means 'acorn', 'Dubois' –'from the woods' and Müller is one of the most common surnames in Germany. Why did you choose 'Siegmund' for the main character? After all, his evolution in this book doesn't match our idea of victory. Are you a pessimist, after all, Mr. Miller?"

"What I meant with his name is that nobody is predestined to victory. Nobody is predestined for anything. We make choices in life, and our choices trigger future events."

"What I've personally understood from the book, is that Siegmund makes moral choices: he gives up his prestigious medical career to take care of his mother and he refuses to participate in the euthanasia programme. But, as a consequence of these choices, he fails. He ends up in a modest hospital, in the middle of nowhere, from which he is sacked in the end. Moreover, suspicions are raised after the war, that he was involved in the Aktion T4 program, though it was within his power to avoid being so. Isn't his failure predestined, after all? His choices seem to be limited. What chance does he have to take the right decision, choosing to be moral or not? Isn't the chance to make choices actually overrated?"

"That's a good point. But we are talking about here are the effects of his own choices. What I mean is that Siegmund, already conscious of these consequences, yet deciding to make the choices he makes. He chose to be moral, so we can't say he failed. He didn't fail as a moral human being, which was his choice. It's not the fate of Oedipus, who slept with his mother, without being aware of it, and this is how he failed."

"Everywhere in this world, since the beginning of humanity, there have been other 'Siegmunds' confronted with similar situations, being in a powerless position of the subordinate, and in that context, forced by their superiors to execute unethical orders, yet also being held responsible, when the regime or the superior falls. Similar situations are probably even more frequent than we think. That raises a moral question, 'How should someone react in this case?' Isn't it just an idealization to think that it is just as simple as refusing to obey those orders? Especially, when it isn't just about counteracting one person, but rather a whole system?"

"I don't think there is a right answer to your question. Sometimes even assiduously made detailed plans have failed to overthrow a system, as in the case of the well-known 'Operation Valkyrie'. What then could a single person, acting alone, do against the whole system? As Siegmund reckoned, even if he killed Hermann, Hermann would have been replaced by another 'Hermann', who would have taken over his job.

"So are you suggesting that for someone in Siegmund's situation, there is no chance of succeeding when it comes to doing the right thing?"

"What I'm trying to say is that a voice can't be heard when a lot of noise is buzzing around."

"What happened to Hermann Wagner? How was it possible for you and Greta to get married?"

"After the war, he was charged with crimes against humanity and executed in 1948."

"Did you see his execution as 'justice'?"

"I would call it 'violent justice'. Whenever circumstances mean we find violence justified, even if we are talking about an act of justice, like in this case, it's only a sign that humanity still has flaws and that we are still not capable of overthrowing our animal side."

"Do you think pity is a sign of moral weakness, as Nietzsche suggested?"

"If 'God is dead', without pity or empathy we'd also be dead. I sometimes wonder myself, if Nietzsche would have lived during the third Reich, and it could have be proven, back then, that he suffered an incurable genetic disease, which would end up in dementia, had he been euthanatized by the Nazi? It's an absurd thought-experiment for us today, but it wouldn't have been so absurd to take this possibility into account back-then. Ironic, isn't it?"

"The character that represents you in this novel reminds me of Viktor Frankl, survivor of the Holocaust and psychiatrist, whose field of interest was 'Logotherapy'; like Joseph the psychologist. Frankl also considered that the primary motivational force of individuals was to give their life meaning. Did he inspire you in your field of research, or in writing this book?"

"No, I didn't even know him in the beginning. It was a joy for me to find out about his work after I started my own research in the same field. It has always been of great happiness to me to find people who think like me, even if I haven't ever met them in person. I would say that maybe that is the reason why I wanted to write books in the first place. It's an opportunity to meet other people's minds, without ever knowing them in person. It's an advantage humanity has."

"Now, Herr Miller, a personal question for you: you said to me that you would like to go on the 'Camino de Santiago', before you die. You're obviously in very good physical condition and still very fit, but you're 93 years old. I haven't heard of anyone your age who have done it. There are young people, who consider it to be a tough task. Why do you want to do this so much?"

"Siegmund and I wanted to do this together in our first year of university, but we didn't find the right moment to do it; there had been the coup d'état in 1933 and the communists had overthrown the monarchy and come to power. In 1935, I fled to France, and then the Second World War broke out, so we no longer had the opportunity to do it together. I want to do this in his memory, for being the best friend I have ever had. If you don't have any more questions for me, may I ask you something too? What are you going to do with Frieda? She's the only character in your novel whose denouement I don't know. Have you thought what you want to do with her?"

"No, actually I haven't, Joseph. Should every story have a denouement? Who knows, maybe I still have one, because her story isn't finished yet. Do you have a suggestion for me, before we say goodbye to each other?"

Joseph smiled.

"Sorry, Christa. I don't have any suggestions anymore. I think you're on your own now, but I'm sure you will find the answers. Just remember, you can reinvent yourself as many times as you wish before you find the path you want to go down. Now we must say goodbye to each other."

After the last interview with Joseph, I prepared a letter to my editor mentioning that all the characters and facts in my novel were pure fiction and I sent it for publication.

Two weeks after my last interview with Joseph, I received an unexpected call. The person at the other end of the line didn't say their name, which irritated me.

"Are you Christa Berg?"

"Yes, who's this?"

"Do you know Joseph? Have you two ever met?"

"Who is this? I think it would be polite to tell me who you are at least, before asking me questions."

The other person laughed.

"Don't worry, Christa, I just want to be sure that you are who you are."

"*You* called me, you know my name, but you're not sure if I am who I am?"

"It's important to be sure that it is you."

"Well, it's me. Who are *you*, and what do you want from me?"

"I'm Joseph's grandson. Now I hope you understand why I wanted to be sure about your identity. My grandfather passed away three days ago. He died in his sleep. He was a lucky man, after all. He didn't want to live any longer, anyway. He was always very independent and wanted to die before he had to depend on someone. I thought you'd want to know. He used to talk a lot about you recently."

"I'm sorry to hear that. He was a dear friend of mine. My condolences. Did he finish his trip to Santiago de Compostela?"

"He died while he was doing it. It was probably too much for his old heart. But he was always a stubborn old goat. It was useless trying to convince him not to do it."

"Well, he was stubborn indeed. But maybe he wouldn't have achieved so much in his life if he hadn't been. You wouldn't have been born otherwise."

"You're right. Look, Christa, I'll be glad to meet you sometime. Just tell me if you ever come to California. You can reach me on this phone number, if you do."

"Aren't you afraid that someone could make a connection between my book and you if I call you?"

"No, not really. I'm sure they've already made the connection. Nothing you've written about is too confidential. If it were confidential, we wouldn't be having this conversation right now."

"Then maybe we'll hear from each other one day, Joseph's grandson. Thanks for letting me know about Joseph. Goodbye."

"Goodbye."

ACKNOWLEDGMENT

I thank S. Geeson for English editing and valuable review.

ABOUT THE AUTHOR

I am a forty-years-old Romanian-born physician, actually a neurologist, living in Germany since 2014.

I have been writing novels, short stories and poems since I was a child. As a student, I was a member of the literary circle of the University of Medicine in Bucharest.

Because of my challenging medical career, I have never found the right time to finish and publish my literary work, until now. However, all the experiences I have had since my childhood: from communism in Romania, my student years, my experience as an immigrant in Spain and Germany- all crystallized in my mind a couple of years ago, when I decided to put them down on paper and publish.

I write literary fiction, but sometimes I like to play with discrete elements of surrealism and expressionism, making the borders between reality and fantasy hazy and allowing the reader to choose the version that fits them most (or to contemplate both).

My first novel, "The journal of a German doctor during the WWII", contemplates philosophical questions about the meaning of life: why some people fail, while others are successful, when playing by the same rules? Should someone be held responsible for carrying out unethical tasks whilst executing orders? How should someone react when forced to undertake an immoral order given by people who possess more power than they have, or represent an authority?

Currently I am writing my second novel, based both on my childhood experiences in communist Romania and my experience as an immigrant in the western world. From these two different perspectives I try to illustrate how capitalism is perceived through the eyes of an immigrant from the ex-communist bloc.

www.ingramcontent.com/pod-product-compliance
Lightning Source LLC
Chambersburg PA
CBHW072223150726
48002CB00005B/1934